Have you read this book ?	

THE HOODED TERROR

A card bearing the silhouette of a cowled head is discovered at numerous crime scenes. The man dubbed the Hooded Terror by the press rules his organization by fear — while within his heart is a greater fear that one day the brother of a man buried in a little cemetery in Devonshire will seek him out and exact vengeance for what happened one dark and stormy night fifteen years ago. Superintendent Trent and DI Cowles set out to learn his secrets and put an end to his evil deeds . . .

Books by Donald Stuart
in the Linford Mystery Library:

MIDNIGHT MURDER
THE WHITE FRIAR
THE MAN IN THE DARK
THE MAN OUTSIDE
THE GREEN PEN MYSTERY

DONALD STUART

THE HOODED TERROR

Complete and Unabridged

LINFORD
Leicester

First published in Great Britain

First Linford Edition
published 2016

A catalogue record for this book is available
from the British Library.

ISBN 978–1–4448–2880–1

Published by
F. A. Thorpe (Publishing)
Anstey, Leicestershire

Set by Words & Graphics Ltd.
Anstey, Leicestershire
Printed and bound in Great Britain by
T. J. International Ltd., Padstow, Cornwall

This book is printed on acid-free paper

1

Introducing Richard Trent

It is an extraordinary fact, but nevertheless a true one, that no one, least of all Richard Trent, can ever be quite certain of the exact date upon which the startling series of crimes and outrages that owed their inception to the mysterious personality, who afterward became known as the Hooded Terror, began.

The organization, which later was to hold London terror-stricken in its grip, started in a small way, slowly and insidiously, like the growth of some malignant disease. There had been several petty crimes, one or two minor robberies, connected only by the fact that in each case had been found the soon to be familiar card bearing the black silhouette of a cowled head. But they passed almost unnoticed, for they were not of sufficient importance to warrant more than a few lines in the newspapers; and it was not until the robbery of the Western and Union Bank in Lombard Street, and the murder of the night watchman, that the world at large became suddenly aware of the terrible menace which had appeared, suddenly and phantom-like, in its midst.

James Lathbury, the managing director of the bank, arrived earlier than usual one morning, to find that someone had saved him the trouble of opening the safe and cleared the strong room of over a quarter of a million sterling. On the stairs lay the body of the watchman, his head and shoulders covered with blood, stone dead, and in his hand a white card bearing the sign of the Hooded Terror.

The police did their best, but there was no clue, not even a fingerprint to go on. Close upon the heels of this followed a second outrage.

Selby P. Doyle, the American cotton millionaire, received a demand for five hundred thousand pounds, the amount to be paid in Treasury notes within seven days. Doyle informed the police. The money was to be sent to an address in the

Haymarket, to a Mr. Smith. It proved to be a newsagent's shop that took in letters for a small fee.

Doyle was advised to send the money, detectives keeping watch for the person who called for it. Nobody came, but two days later, after a particularly heavy day in the city, Selby Doyle returned to his house in the country; and after dinner, following his usual custom, he strolled out into the grounds to smoke a cigar.

At 10.30, the butler, finding that his master had not returned, went in search of him. He found him lying by a small gate leading into a covert. His head had been beaten in and he was stone dead. In his hand was the familiar card, while scrawled across it in pencil ran the message: 'It is better to pay'.

Many similar outrages happened, and in several cases wealthy men, remembering the fate that had overtaken Selby Doyle, paid up.

The police were at their wits' end. Once or twice they managed to pull in one or two of the minor members of the gang, but they either could not, or were in too great a fear of the consequences to give any information concerning the identity of their mysterious leader.

Each one told the same story. They had never seen the head of the gang; their instructions reached them by telephone, the message emanating from one public call office and being received at another, where they were instructed to be at a certain time. Written instructions they found in their pockets without knowing how they got there.

And so the wave of terror spread over London, and no man knew who was going to be the next victim, or whether he would wake one morning to find a card bearing the black silhouette on his breakfast table.

Month after month passed, and during that time scarcely a week went by without the newspapers splashing in flaring headlines some further exploit of the Hooded Terror. And all the while, like a monstrous spider in the centre of his web-like organization, merciless and without pity, was the man who, unknown and shrouded in mystery, controlled with an

4

iron hand the puppets he had collected round him to do his bidding. He ruled by fear, while within his heart was a greater fear, a fear that one day the brother of a certain man lying stark and cold in a little cemetery in Devonshire would seek him out and, having found him, exact vengeance for what had happened one dark and stormy night fifteen years ago.

Towards the close of a dull October afternoon, Richard Trent, the young superintendent of police, sat at his big desk in his large bare room that overlooked the Thames Embankment, staring idly at the blotting pad in front of him. His forehead was puckered up into a thoughtful frown; his youthful and usually cheery face wore a worried expression.

Outside, the fog, which was later to descend upon London, blotting out every landmark like a sponge drawn across a slate, was as yet but a grey misty threat of the dense blanket of yellow vapour that was to come.

Here and there, where the fitful gleam of a street lamp cast a dim and murky splash of radiance, a shapeless figure seemed to detach itself occasionally from the enveloping mist, loom for a moment in the light, and vanish the next instant; and, phantom-like, become once more part of the surrounding fog which had given it birth.

Big Ben boomed out the hour of six, and the sound of the great bell roused Trent from his reverie. He stretched out his hand to stir the long-neglected cup of tea that stood at his elbow. It was stone cold, as he presently found when he sipped at its contents; with a grimace of disgust he pushed the cup from him and, rising to his feet, crossed to the window and stared gloomily out at the mist-swathed river.

But the river was not nearly as foggy as Dick Trent's mind. The Hooded Terror was getting on his nerves. For the past eight months he had devoted the whole of his time to rounding up the gang, but so far without a vestige of success.

The newspapers were beginning to publish fairly broad hints as to the inefficiency of the police, and their editorials were becoming direct, almost to the point of offensiveness. One openly stated that police headquarters needed a thorough overhauling, and the introducing of new blood to cope with the menace. Only that morning Dick had had a particularly unpleasant interview with the assistant commissioner, an individual who possessed ideas of his own and was not diffident in expressing them in most un-parliamentary language.

Something had to be done, and done soon, for the whole country was getting in a panic. There came a tap at the door, and as Dick growled out an invitation Inspector Cowles entered the room.

Anyone less like the popular idea of a detective it would have been almost impossible to have found. From the top of his immaculate silk hat to the soles of his small, beautifully polished patent leather shoes, he radiated the atmosphere of the lazy club lounger — the wealthy man of leisure. The white gardenia, which he invariably wore in his buttonhole, had become a standing joke at Scotland Yard; but in spite of his almost effeminate appearance, Dick Trent knew that there was not a cleverer man in the whole of the police force than Detective-Inspector John Cowles of the C.I.D.

Cowles removed his glossy hat as he advanced into the room and laid it carefully on a side table, together with light gloves.

'Well,' said Dick as he seated himself and waved Cowles into another chair, 'any luck?'

That immaculate man sat down, taking great care to avoid spoiling the crease in his trousers. 'I've seen Phrynne,' he answered, and he spoke with a drawl and a slight lisp, 'and I think he'll come across. He wants to see you tonight, at your flat. It took a lot of persuasion even to make him go as far as that. The poor beggar seems scared to death.'

'And you really think he knows something?' asked Dick, lighting a cigarette and offering his case to his companion.

'He wrenched open the door and almost stumbled over the figure lying on the step.' Inspector Cowles carefully selected a cigarette, tapping it daintily on his fingernail. 'If what he says is true,' he replied when it was alight to his satisfaction, 'he knows the real identity of the Hooded Terror.'

'And he's prepared to squeal?'

'On the condition that he gets the reward and we guarantee his personal safely,' said Cowles. 'I said just now that Phrynne is about the most badly frightened man I've met for some time; and if half the stories about our mysterious friend are true, he's got good reason for being so.'

'He hasn't been out of prison long,' said Trent thoughtfully.

'Eight months,' answered Inspector Cowles. 'Got seven years for blackmail. The Hooded Terror met him almost at the prison gates and got him to join the gang. That's how he has enlisted most of his recruits.'

'Well, I only hope that Phrynne is speaking the truth and can give us a line to the Terror,' said Dick. 'This thing's getting beyond being annoying, Cowles. It is becoming impossible. Did you see the papers this morning?'

Cowles nodded shortly. 'Hot air,' he

said briefly. 'They've got to write about something, and this gives them a subject. I'd like to put some of them in our shoes and see what sort of a show they'd make. There's only one who'd do any good, and that's young Morrison of the *Monitor*. He's a bright lad.'

There was a tap at the door, and a sergeant entered with some reports for Dick to sign. He hastily read them through and appended his signature, and when the man had gone, rose to his feet with a sigh of weariness.

'I'm going home,' he announced. 'You might as well come along and dine with me, then you'll be on hand to hear what Phrynne has to say. What time is he coming?'

'He said between seven-thirty and eight,' replied Inspector Cowles, rising from his chair and flicking an imaginary speck of dust from his well-brushed coat sleeve.

Dick Trent was pulling on his overcoat when an exclamation from his companion made him look in Cowles's direction. The immaculate inspector had taken a snowy handkerchief from his breast pocket and in doing so had jerked out a square white envelope which fell to the floor. Cowles picked it up, staring at it in blank surprise; then with his thumb he ripped open the flap and withdrew the contents — a small square of thin pasteboard.

'Well, I'm damned!' he exclaimed, and handed it to Dick.

It bore neither date nor address, but the message was scrawled across it in pencil. It ran: 'Leave me alone and I'll leave you alone, otherwise — ' Beneath was the stamped impression of a black-cowled head.

'Well, what do you think of it?' asked the inspector. 'How the devil it got into my pocket is a mystery.'

Dick shrugged his shoulders. 'Someone slipped it there while you were out,' he answered. 'A clever pick-pocket could do it with ease, and this Hooded Terror numbers many among his associates. It's no good testing it for fingerprints — there never are any.' He handed the card back to Cowles, and the latter slipped it into his notebook.

They descended the stairs and passed beneath the big arch which leads on to the Embankment. The fog had thickened, and although it was still possible to see fairly clearly, Dick decided it would be quicker to travel to Sloane Street by Tube than by taxi.

They turned westward and walked along in the direction of Charing Cross; a taxi that had been waiting drawn up by the kerb began to follow slowly in their wake.

'There's one thing,' remarked Cowles, breaking the silence at length. 'If the Hooded Terror thinks he's going to start scaring Scotland Yard with his theatrical warnings, he's going to get a shock. He's clever, but not all-powerful. There are some things he cannot do. I — ' He broke off with a sharp exclamation. He had trodden on a piece of orange peel left by some careless person lying on the pavement, and slipping, cannoned into Dick Trent, almost knocking him off his feet.

The accident saved his life, for at the same instant from behind the taxi came two sharp reports, and Dick felt the wind of the bullets as they whistled past his head and thudded on the wall beside him. The taxi was out of sight before a policeman, who heard the shots, came running up.

'They certainly work swiftly,' remarked Inspector Cowles coolly, as he gazed at the wall of fog into which the car had vanished.

2

The Silencing of Blackie Phrynne

Jack Morrison, better known to his friends as 'Last Minute' Morrison, descended hurriedly from the taxicab that had borne him from Fleet Street at a snail's pace, and, paying the driver, pressed hard and continuously at the bell of Richard Trent's flat in Sloane Street.

He had earned his soubriquet throughout the 'Street of Ink' from the fact that he never, by any chance, turned in his 'copy' until literally the last available moment. There was a story that may or may not be true of how, during a murder case, Morrison had dashed into the office of the *Daily Monitor* just after the paper had gone to press, and in order to save time detailed his story direct to the linotype operator. It was probably an exaggeration, but it was just the kind of thing that Last Minute Morrison was capable of doing.

A short, youthful-looking fair-haired man, his most attractive features were his eyes. They shone with the enjoyment of life, and possessed a magnetic quality that forced even the gloomiest of people to respond to the merry twinkle that lurked in their depths.

Dick's servant, Albert Coates, opened the door and smiled as he recognized the visitor. 'I'm afraid Mr. Trent is not in, sir,' he said, 'but he phoned a few minutes ago saying that he would be back to dinner. Perhaps you would care to wait?'

'Wait? I'm always waiting, but nothing ever turns up,' answered Morrison, his voice seeming to quiver with suppressed amusement. 'The man who said 'Everything comes to him who waits' must have been in the hotel business.'

He was following Coates up the stairs while he was talking, for Dick's flat was on the third floor. The servant showed him into the comfortable sitting room. A cosy fire was burning in the grate and the table was set for two.

'Hello,' said Morrison as his sharp eyes

lighted on the second plate, 'who is to be the guest? Am I spoiling some youthful romance by becoming what is generally known as the gooseberry?'

'I don't think so, sir,' replied Albert, smiling. 'I believe Mr. Trent is bringing Inspector Cowles back to dinner with him.'

Morrison settled himself in a deep armchair, and presently Albert appeared bearing a tray containing a decanter, syphon, and glasses, which he set down on a small table by the visitor's side.

Jack Morrison mixed himself a whisky and soda, and producing a gold cigarette case from the hip pocket of his trousers, selected a cigarette. Having lighted it, he lay back in the chair with a sigh of contentment. It was seldom that he found time to relax, and fully appreciated the chance of a lazy half-hour that presented itself.

The warmth of the room and the comfort of the armchair presently began to have a drowsy effect on his senses, and his eyes closed. The cigarette, burning down and scorching his fingers, woke him with a start. Almost at the same moment Dick Trent and Inspector Cowles came into the room.

'Hello, you lazy devil,' said Dick with a smile as he caught sight of the recumbent figure in the chair. 'How did you get here?'

'By taxi. I'm here on business, Dick.'

'I didn't know you ever did any,' said Trent, smiling. 'Have you dined?'

Morrison nodded. 'Knowing your extraordinary ideas of hospitality, I had a hasty chop before I came on here,' he replied. 'But you and Cowles carry on. I can talk while you eat — that is, after you've got through the soup,' he added with a grin.

Albert entered with a tray. After he had withdrawn, and Dick and Cowles were comfortably seated at the table, Morrison continued: 'Old Tiles, my editor at the *Monitor*, has come to the conclusion that it is time someone put a stop to this Hooded Terror scare, and he's detailed me for the job.'

Dick Trent's eyes twinkled as he crumbled his bread. 'This is where you start enjoying yourself, Jack,' he remarked pleasantly. 'They nearly got Cowles half an hour ago; and when they find that you've butted into the game, if they don't know it already, they'll most likely include you in their amiable attentions.'

Morrison looked up sharply. 'Nearly got Cowles — when?' he asked.

Dick related the experience on the Embankment, and when he had finished, Morrison whistled softly. 'They certainly seem to mean business,' he said. 'I'd give something to know the real identity of the Hooded Terror.'

'So would a good many people — myself included,' said the immaculate Cowles. 'And when he is revealed, we're all going to get a shock.'

Morrison looked at him curiously. 'You sound as though you know something,' he remarked.

Cowles laid down his spoon and shrugged. 'I know no more than anyone else,' he replied, 'but I've made a specialty of the Hooded Terror crimes and, if I didn't know that the thing was impossible, because the man's been dead for nearly fifteen years, I'd say that the Hooded Terror was Hammer Stevens.'

'Hammer Stevens? He was murdered, wasn't he?' asked Dick.

'That's why I say it is an impossibility,' answered Inspector Cowles. 'But it's the sort of thing that would have appealed to Stevens. He always liked to put a touch of the theatrical in his work.'

'I've read about the case in some of the back files of the *Monitor*,' said Last Minute Morrison. 'Stevens was killed by a man named Arkwright, wasn't he?'

Cowles nodded. 'Arkwright was a friend of his. We always believed he was a fence on a big scale, but we could never pull anything on him. He lived in a rambling old house on the edge of Dartmoor, almost within sight of the prison. Stevens was serving a sentence for robbery with violence — hit his victim over the head; it was a favorite trick of his, and earned him his soubriquet of 'Hammer'. One night, during a storm, he escaped from the prison and made his way to Arkwright's house. What happened there we shall never know, but the following morning the warders found Stevens's body lying in the hall. He had been killed with a shotgun fired at close range. I believe he was a pretty ghastly sight. Arkwright had disappeared.'

'He never was found, was he?' asked Morrison.

'No,' answered Cowles. 'He vanished completely, and has never been heard of from that day to this.'

At that moment there came an interruption from Albert to inform Dick that there was someone on the phone for him. And with a word of apology, Trent left the room.

He returned in a few minutes. 'It was Blackie Phrynne,' he announced to Cowles. 'He was phoning from a call office, and says he'll be along here in five minutes.'

'Who is Blackie Phrynne?' asked Morrison curiously.

'Blackie Phrynne,' replied Dick, attacking the grilled steak that the servant had brought in during his absence, 'is a member of the Hooded Terror gang who, dazzled by the reward, has decided to squeal. Whether he knows anything or not remains to be seen. He says that he has discovered the identity of the mysterious leader of the gang.'

'And is in a state almost bordering on collapse, through fear that the Hooded Terror may discover his intention of peaching,' put in Inspector Cowles. 'I hate dealing with a squealer, but in some cases it is necessary.'

'If this man, Phrynne, is speaking the truth,' said Jack Morrison, 'the quest for the Hooded Terror will be at an end.'

Dick nodded. 'It sounds almost too good to be true, doesn't it?'

The front door bell pealed insistently. 'That's Blackie,' said Dick, and almost on top of his words there came from below a shrill, terror-laden scream — a scream that ended abruptly, like the sudden snapping of a thread.

In an instant, his face set and grim, Dick Trent leapt to his feet and went racing down the stairs, followed by Inspector Cowles and Jack Morrison.

He wrenched open the front door and

almost stumbled over the figure lying on the step. It was Blackie Phrynne, and he was stone dead, the knife that had killed him still protruding from between his shoulder blades.

The fog had thinned in that unaccountable way that fogs have, and by the kerb opposite the door a taxi stood, its engine still running slowly. The driver had descended from his seat and was standing, trembling, on the pavement by the side of his cab.

'I see'd it happen, guv'nor,' he quavered in a scared voice. 'The gent 'ad paid me and 'ad just rung the bell, when a man jumped out of the shadders of the next doorway and stuck a knife in his back, and ran. 'E was gone almost before I knew what 'ad 'appened.' He pointed down the street.

A constable came running up, and a little knot of spectators began to collect from nowhere, as is the habit of a London crowd. 'What's happened, sir?' asked the policeman.

Dick made known his identity and briefly explained. 'The man's stone dead,' he said. 'You'd better fetch an ambulance.' The constable saluted and hurried away.

'You wait,' continued Trent, turning to the frightened cab driver. 'We shall want you later.' The man nodded reluctantly.

Inspector Cowles was bending over the body. Presently he turned it gently over, and as he did so he saw something — a white object that had been lying underneath. It was a small card, and bore below a penciled scrawl — the silhouette of a hooded head in black. Without a word he handed it to Dick, and in the light of the hill lamp Trent read the penciled words written on the face of the card: 'A lesson — and a warning to others!'

Inspector Cowles rose to his feet and carefully dusted the knees of his trousers, then he looked at Dick with a rueful smile. 'I think this proves that Blackie was not lying when he said he knew the Hooded Terror,' he said grimly. 'He knew — and the knowledge cost him his life.'

The ambulance arrived with a clanging of bells, scattering the group of morbid sightseers on the kerb, and with it the divisional surgeon. His examination was brief.

'The knife entered the heart, severing the left ventricle,' he said. 'Death must have been instantaneous.'

The remains of poor Blackie Phrynne were lifted into the ambulance, and it drove off on its way to the mortuary.

'Now,' said Dick, 'where's that taxi driver? We'd better get his name and address — he'll be wanted as a witness at the inquest.'

But the taxi driver had disappeared, although no one had seen him go. His cab still remained at the kerb, but the driver had vanished; and search as they might, he could not be found.

Dick Trent turned to Cowles with a gesture of despair. 'I might have known,' he said bitterly.

'Known what?' asked Last Minute Morrison, an interested spectator.

'The cab driver was the Hooded Terror himself,' said Trent, and turned away to speak to the policeman.

3

Mr. Lathbury's Secretary

Christine Baker woke to the shrill summons of the alarm clock on the little table by her side, and surveyed the morning, or as much of it as could be seen through the window of her tiny bedroom, with sleep-laden eyes. The fog of the previous night had vanished and given place to a sharp frost, and the morning, although cold and raw, was bright and sunny.

For a few moments she lay still while the mists of sleep cleared from her brain; and then, seeing that the time was getting on for half-past eight, sprang out of bed, and drawing a dressing gown about her slim shoulders, made her way into the little kitchenette and put a kettle on the gas stove. By the time she had taken her bath the kettle was boiling, and she made herself a cup of tea.

She was slim of build, straight as a plummet-line from chin to toe, and she carried herself with dignity. Her face was Madonna-like in its purity, but a blue-eyed, cherry-lipped Madonna, vital and challenging. She was a bud of a girl breaking into the summer bloom of maturity. The sensitive mouth, with its full, red lips; the round, girlish chin; and the satin-white throat and velvety skin, unmarked or blemished by paint or artifice, were the gifts of youth that constituted her charm. The spun gold of her hair, cut short at the back to show the line of her well-shaped head, strayed over her forehead into little rebellious curls, which she pushed back now and again with a small hand as, having dressed, she set about preparing her breakfast.

Christine lived in a tiny mansion flat a stone's throw from Piccadilly Circus. At half-past nine she left the flat and walked briskly to Piccadilly Circus, where she stood waiting for a bus to take her to Moorgate Street.

Richard Trent, on his way to Scotland

Yard, saw her; and, stopping, raised his hat, a look of pleasure on his face. 'This is a surprise,' he said, smiling down at the girl. 'You are the last person I expected to see round this way.'

'You can't pass this way often then at this hour, Mr. Trent,' answered Christine, laughing, 'or else you would know that I'm always here at nine-thirty.'

Dick had met the girl during his investigation of the robbery at Lathbury's bank, the first big outrage that had brought the Hooded Terror into prominence; and although usually fairly indifferent as far as women were concerned, he had been more than casually interested in this slim girl with the big blue eyes. 'How is everything with the banking world?' he asked.

He spoke jocularly, but Christine noticed the drawn look on his face and the dark rings round his eyes that spoke plainly of worry and sleepless nights. 'I don't think we are likely to suspend payment or anything like that for a day or two,' she replied in the same tone. 'And how is Scotland Yard?'

'Fine,' answered Dick, without enthusiasm. 'The chief commissioner is thinking of having it turned into a residential hotel for the convenience of the Hooded Terror and his gang.'

The girl's smile faded and her face went suddenly pale. 'Mr. Trent,' she said seriously, 'do you think he'll ever be caught?'

'If by 'he' you mean the Hooded Terror,' replied Dick, 'I should say yes. He's clever, extraordinarily clever, but all criminals make a slip sooner or later. He's been longer making it than most of 'em, that's all.'

'I hope you're right,' said the girl. 'Here comes my bus,' she added. 'Goodbye, Mr. Trent.' She boarded the crowded bus and ran lightly up the stairs to the only vacant seat on the top. She looked back as they rounded the corner, and waved her hand as she saw Dick's tall figure, still standing looking after her; and for the first time in her life, she felt reluctant to analyze her feelings concerning the young man.

For the rest of the journey she remained lost in thought, and it was with a start of surprise that she suddenly realized that she had reached her destination.

Mr. James Lathbury had already arrived when she got to the bank. He had a trick of getting there early, and Christine had barely taken off her hat and coat in a little room that adjoined his office before his bell rang, summoning her into his presence.

Lathbury was a stout, somewhat pompous man of something between forty and fifty. It was quite impossible to guess his correct age, for although his hair was sparse and grey, his face, big and full and double-chinned, was free from lines and smooth as a boy's. He affected a certain smartness of dress and wore a rimless monocle that no one had ever seen out of his eye.

As she entered he looked up from his desk, on which lay a pile of newly opened correspondence, and greeted her with a peculiar smile. Whereas in repose his large face was smooth and seamless, when he smiled it broke up into innumerable lines and wrinkles, and always reminded

Christine of a monstrous crab apple.

'Good morning, Miss Baker,' he said pleasantly. 'A fine morning; cold, but invigorating, yes — invigorating. I see by the papers that the Hooded Terror has committed another atrocious crime. There is a full account of it in the *Monitor*. Their reporter apparently was an eyewitness. Really, the man's audacity is amazing!'

He paused as if he had just given utterance to a most profound statement, and was allowing time for his words to sink in and take effect. 'The murder this time was actually committed on the very doorstep of a superintendent of police's residence. Superintendent Trent,' went on Mr. Lathbury. 'It is disgraceful that they cannot cope with this menace, which is striking at the root of civilization.'

Christine experienced a sensation as though a cold hand had closed around her heart, and she felt the blood recede from her face. A voice — her own voice, but sounding far off and faint — reached her ears. 'Who — who was killed?' she asked tremulously.

Mr. Lathbury picked up an open paper

from the desk and held it in a chubby hand. 'A man named Blackie Phrynne,' he answered. 'He was a criminal. These people have extraordinary names. It appears that he was a member of the gang, but had decided to turn informer on account of the reward. He had discovered the real identity of this criminal, and was preparing to tell the police all he knew. They had a wonderful chance, but bungled it, and allowed the man to be murdered on their very doorstep. I certainly agree with the papers that most drastic steps should be taken immediately, and the police force thoroughly reorganized.'

The girl made no reply; she was thinking of Richard Trent and his pale face and dark-circled eyes. No wonder he looked ill and tired out.

'As long as this criminal is allowed to remain at large,' continued the banker, 'it is impossible for any respectable citizen to feel secure. I'm not naturally a nervous man — ' Christine smiled inwardly, for there had been an occasion when Mr. Lathbury had enlisted the services of the entire staff to deal with a mouse that had intruded into his private office. ' — but I confess that since the robbery of the bank and my discovery of poor Walters on the stairs, my nerves have been a complete wreck.'

'You should see a doctor,' said the girl.

'I have consulted several,' replied Mr. Lathbury, 'and have consumed a vast quantity of medicine, but it has done me no good. The last doctor informed me that I lived too much alone, and advised me to seek more bright and congenial society. In short, he — er, suggested that I should marry.' He stopped, and his hand, straying nervously about the desk, picked up a pencil and started drawing innumerable little circles on the blotting pad.

Christine knew this little habit of old, and knew that it denoted that the stout banker was thinking deeply. For some time Lathbury remained silent, and the girl waited, wondering what was coming next; twice during the interval he opened his mouth as though about to speak, but closed it again without the words being uttered. He had apparently forgotten that

32

she was still standing, which was unlike him, for usually Lathbury was the essence of politeness. Without waiting for permission, she sat down in her usual chair opposite him on the other side of the big desk.

The movement seemed to rouse him from his reverie, for he continued where he had left off. 'I have for some weeks been considering relinquishing the state of — er — single blessedness,' he said. 'I have amassed a considerable amount of — shall we say worldly goods, and I am by no means an old man — the disparity in our ages is not in these days an insurmountable obstacle. I would endeavor to do all in my power to make you — er, happy.' He paused.

Christine sat stunned, and it was some minutes before she could think of a suitable reply, for Lathbury was obviously waiting for her to speak. 'Is this a proposal?' she managed to gasp at length.

The banker nodded ponderously. 'No doubt it has come as rather a shock to you,' he said. 'I flatter myself that I have managed to conceal my feelings for you up till now. Possibly you have never looked upon me in the light of a husband, but I have given a lot of thought to the matter, and I can see no reason why this should not be — yes, should not be.'

He spoke as though he were reciting a carefully rehearsed speech; and if the bank itself had suddenly fallen down and collapsed about her ears, the girl could not have been more astonished. She could only gaze at him open-eyed, scarcely believing the evidence of her senses.

'But — Mr. Lathbury,' she stammered, and her throat had gone so suddenly dry that she found difficulty in getting her words out, 'I had no idea — '

'There is no need for you to decide in a hurry — er — Christine,' said Lathbury. 'I quite realize that — er — the suddenness of my proposal has for the moment — er — taken your breath away. But take your time and — er — think it over — yes, think it over.'

'It's very kind of you,' she answered, 'and, of course, I feel . . . ' She hesitated. ' . . . honored, but I'm afraid it's impossible. I don't want to marry you. I don't want to marry anybody.'

'I never expected — I never hoped that you would consent immediately,' said Mr. Lathbury. 'All I want you to do is to consider it — er — at your leisure, and not to be hasty — no, not to be hasty.'

Christine was saved the embarrassment of a reply by a tap on the door and the appearance of Jackson, one of the clerks, with a card. Mr. Lathbury looked at him with a frown and waved his hand in protest. 'I really cannot see anybody. I'm extremely busy. Who is it?' he asked sharply.

'A Mr. Harold Stepping, sir,' answered the clerk. 'He wishes to see you about opening an account at the bank.' He laid the card on the desk, and James Lathbury picked it up, then twirled it about in his fat hand hesitantly.

'Oh, well, I'll see him,' he said shortly.

Christine welcomed the interruption, for it gave her time to think and recover from the shock of the banker's proposal. She passed Mr. Stepping as she left the inner office. Beyond the fact that he was tall and rather plainly dressed, she scarcely noticed him; and even if she had, he certainly would have meant nothing to her.

Had Richard Trent, at that precise moment in close conversation with Inspector Cowles, been there, however, it would have been a different matter. For Mr. Stepping figured largely in the Record Office at Scotland Yard under the name of 'Sparkler' Wallace and several other aliases, while written beneath in a neat hand in red ink was the word 'Dangerous'.

4

The Man Who Watched

Mr. James Lathbury, having completed his day's business, stepped into his big car at the door of the bank and sank back into its luxurious cushions with a sigh of relief. During the journey home to his house, in Grosvenor Place, he allowed his mind to wander aimlessly over the events of the day. Occupying the foremost place in his thoughts was Christine Baker.

He had not expected the girl to accept his offer of marriage at once, but he possessed a sufficient amount of personal vanity to believe that, with careful handling, she would eventually consent. With half-closed eyes he lay back and speculated pleasantly on the future.

It was not generally known, but Mr. Lathbury practically owned the Western and Union Bank. Entering the business as manager some years previously, at a time when the bank was almost on the verge of being insolvent, he had, by sheer financial ability, pulled it through the crisis, and at the same time acquired the bulk of the shares.

In the city of London the Western and Union Bank was respected without being considered. It was a survival of one of those private banking corporations that had come into existence in the early part of the eighteenth century, and had successfully resisted the encroachments of the great joint stock companies. Its business under the skilful handling of James Lathbury was fairly prosperous, and its clientele extremely select. At times enormous sums passed through its books.

The limousine drew up at the banker's house, and Mr. Lathbury alighted.

His middle-aged, ultra-respectable butler was waiting in the hall to help him off with his coat; and after his usual remark upon the state of the weather, Mr. Lathbury ascended to his study on the first floor, to read the evening paper until it was time for his dinner.

Starting with the financial column and

city notes, it was his usual custom to work steadily through the papers until he had exhausted their contents and kept himself thoroughly up to date regarding the latest news of the day. But tonight his thoughts wandered from the printed pages before him; and try as he would, he could not prevent the vision of a girl's face set in a frame of spun-gold hair, and two limpid blue eyes that seemed to stare steadfastly into his own, from intruding itself between his gaze and the paper he was trying to read.

He gave it up at last and, throwing down the papers, rose from his seat and strolled over to the window, looking out upon the quiet square.

A strange fit of restlessness utterly unusual to his nature had got him in its grip, and it was with a feeling of relief that he descended to his dining room when Wills, the butler, announced that dinner was ready.

The big room, furnished heavily in old oak, seemed to look unusually spacious and empty, and the solitary plate set at one end of the large table, lonelier than it had ever done before.

With a suppressed sigh, the banker sat down. The dinner was carefully chosen and beautifully cooked and served, for Lathbury was something of an epicure and believed in the good things of life. But tonight for some reason he seemed to have lost his appetite, and each dish was sent away scarcely touched.

When the meal was finished, the banker ordered coffee to be brought to his study and returned upstairs, where he seated himself at his desk and occupied some time in writing letters.

Having finished his coffee and also his correspondence, he glanced at his watch, descended to the hall, and was helped into his coat.

Passing out into the rain-soaked street, he looked round for a taxi. There was not one in sight, and Lathbury had to walk to the end of the street before he found a vacant vehicle.

A tall man in a light raincoat who had been watching the house from the other side of the roadway moved slowly in his wake, and was in time to hear the directions given to the driver. He stood for some time after the banker had driven off, watching the receding tail-lamp of the taxi. Then he returned and walked slowly back to the place whence he had come, chuckling softly to himself; for Mr. Harold Stepping, better known as Sparkler Wallace, had stumbled upon a fact out of which he thought he saw a way of putting a considerable amount of money into his own pocket, a state of affairs which always had the effect of causing Mr. Stepping the most profound enjoyment.

With his mind full of rosy dreams for the future, and oblivious of the inclemency of the night, Mr. Stepping swung off at a fair pace and made his way in the direction of Victoria. He turned in at the approach to the station and, after glancing at his watch, entered a buffet and ordered himself a whisky and soda. When the girl behind the bar had patted her hair into what she considered was a becoming position, and condescended to serve him, Mr. Stepping drained his glass at a gulp and ordered another, for his vigil outside James Lathbury's house had chilled him and he was glad of the stimulant.

After his second drink, he left the bar and sought a public call office. Having assured himself that the door behind him was securely closed and therefore that no word of his could possibly be overheard by the outside world, he gave a number to the exchange, and waited.

Presently a woman's voice came to him over the wire. It was a shrill, unmusical voice, but at the same time not without a certain charm of its own. 'Who is that?' it demanded.

'Is that you, Lydia?' asked Mr. Stepping unnecessarily. 'It's Harry speaking. Listen. Can you meet me in half an hour? Under the clock at Victoria?'

'I'm not dressed, and it's a beastly night,' demurred Lydia. 'What's the great idea, anyhow?'

'I can't tell you over the phone,' said Stepping impatiently, 'but it's important. Slip into something and come along.'

'All right,' she replied without enthusiasm. 'I'll get there as soon as I can.'

'That's a good girl,' said Mr. Stepping, and rang off.

To while away the time he strolled over to the Continental side of the station, and stood watching the little groups of people waiting to meet friends or relations from the boat-train. Humanity in all its varying types possessed a great interest to Mr. Stepping, and in no place is there presented a better chance of studying one's fellow creatures than the platform of a London railway station. Every grade and every class can be found jostling elbows.

Mr. Stepping had just spotted a pick-pocket acquaintance of his, and was watching his movements with that feeling of superiority that every big crook feels towards his lesser confrere, when a touch on his arm caused him to swing round. To a man of Mr. Stepping's occupation there is always something disturbing about a sudden touch on the arm.

'Hello, Harry,' drawled a lisping voice. 'What are you doing here?'

The immaculate Inspector Cowles stood at his elbow clad in a beautifully cut over-coat, which being open displayed the faultless evening dress beneath. In his buttonhole was the inevitable white gardenia.

'Oh, it's you,' said Mr. Stepping in a voice without a touch of cordiality in its tone. 'See here, Cowles, I'm doing nothing that concerns you.'

'Everything you do concerns me,' answered Cowles pleasantly. 'What's the game now, Harry?'

'There's no game at all,' said Stepping in an injured voice. 'Can't a fellow wait for a friend without half Scotland Yard butting in?'

'I'm inclined to take that as a compliment,' said Inspector Cowles. 'Who would you refer to as the other half of Scotland Yard? By the way, how is the fair Lydia?'

Mr. Stepping regarded him silently for a moment. 'Lydia?' he asked in a perplexed voice. 'Who is Lydia?'

'Come, come, Harry,' said Cowles with a smile, 'you know very well whom I mean. Your charming wife, Mrs. Wallace. Or did you marry her in one of your other names?'

'It appears to me, Cowles, you know a *lot* about my private affairs,' snarled the other.

'It's a hobby of mine — people's *private* affairs,' answered the inspector, lighting a cigarette.

'It's a hobby that'll land you into a lot of trouble,' retorted Stepping. 'You look out, Cowles. There's something coming to you that you won't like, and it is coming soon. You've been sticking your head into a hornet's nest lately, and the hornet's out to sting you. My advice is — quit.' He turned on his heel and walked away, leaving Inspector Cowles staring after him, a thoughtful expression on his face.

Mr. Stepping had scarcely been waiting by the clock for more than ten minutes when he saw the smart figure of his wife approaching from the main entrance to the station. Their marriage had been a peculiar one, for they had been married secretly and had never lived together. At Lydia Stepping's flat in Victoria Street she was known as Miss Benson, and Stepping never by any chance called there, and ordinarily they passed each other in the street as strangers. But in all Stepping's schemes his wife was his only confidant,

45

and on more than one occasion success had been won by her shrewdness and quick foresight. The mere fact that they were never seen together made her all the more useful when she had to play the role of decoy, which she did on many occasions.

She was small and dainty, with a perfect figure, and her face wore a perpetual look of childlike innocence. There was a touch of hardness, however, about her large grey eyes, and an expression that would have told a student of psychology that Lydia Stepping was not quite so unsophisticated as she looked. But Lydia made it a habit to steer clear of students of psychology.

As she approached, Mr. Stepping gave an almost imperceptible sign and strolled over to the booking office. The girl made in the same direction and was close enough to hear him take a first-class ticket to a destination some miles down the line. She bought a similar ticket, and they both strolled onto the platform.

A train was in and Stepping selected an empty first-class carriage and got in. After a little while the girl got into the same compartment. But it was not until the train had started and drawn clear of the station that they spoke to each other. It had been Stepping who had devised this method of communication, and it certainly possessed the advantage of privacy; for if anyone got in, they instantly became strangers once more.

'Well, Harry,' said the girl, 'what's all the excitement? I suppose you've got some new scheme on hand?'

'You're right, my dear,' he said with a smile, offering Lydia a cigarette. 'And it's going to be the last. We can retire on the proceeds.'

She accepted a light from the match he held out to her, and blew out a wreath of smoke. 'Tell me all about it,' she said, shortly; and for over half an hour Mr. Stepping talked, his wife's eyes opening wider and wider and wider with astonishment as he proceeded.

5

The Handkerchief

It seemed to Richard Trent that his head had scarcely touched the pillow before the shrill ringing of the telephone bell at his beside woke him with a start.

It was after two when he had gone to bed; as he sleepily lifted the receiver, he glanced at the travelling clock that stood by the little table, and saw by the luminous dial that it was nearly half past four.

'Hello,' he said, yawning into the mouthpiece. 'Who's that?'

A man's voice, very agitated, answered him over the wire. 'Is that you, Mr., Trent?' it asked. 'This is Lathbury speaking — James Lathbury. There has been a robbery at my house, in Grosvenor Place. We nearly caught the man, but, unfortunately, he got away — yes, got away.' There was a quiver in the banker's voice that was not solely due to agitation, but held a trace of fear in its tone.

'Why did you phone me?' asked Dick irritably, and not unreasonably annoyed at being wakened in the middle of the night. 'You should have communicated direct with the police.'

'I thought you'd be interested,' answered Lathbury. 'It's the work of the Hooded Terror!'

Dick instantly became alert. 'How do you know that?' he asked quickly.

'He left his usual sign,' replied Mr. Lathbury. 'Left it upon the desk in my study. Really, the audacity of the man is beyond anything I could have imagined.'

'Right,' said Dick. 'I will come along at once. See that nothing is disturbed until I get there.'

He hung up the receiver, cutting off the banker's protestations of thanks. Shouting for Albert, he hurriedly dressed while the sleepy-eyed servant prepared hot coffee. Waiting only to gulp down a cup of the steaming fluid, Dick left the flat and went in search of a taxi. It was some time before he was lucky enough to find a belated cab and, stepping in, was driven quickly to Grosvenor Square.

The banker's house was brilliantly lit, and as the taxi drew up at the door it opened. The figure of Wills the butler — which presented a ludicrous appearance, dressed partially in pajamas and partially in his habitual black attire — came out to the top of the steps to meet him.

'Mr. Lathbury is in the dining room, sir,' he announced. 'It's a shocking affair.' Dick nodded shortly and made his way to the dining room.

The stout figure of Lathbury, clad in a brilliant silk dressing gown that he had evidently slipped on over his night attire, was seated by the table sipping a cup of tea. The hand that held the cup was trembling, and Dick checked a smile as he caught the expression on the banker's chubby face. Evidently Mr. Lathbury had received a severe shock.

'Well,' he said as he entered and, refusing the banker's offer of refreshment, seated himself in a chair on the other side of the table, 'tell me all about it.'

'I know very little — very little, indeed. I spent the evening at my club, but feeling a little indisposed, left earlier than usual and retired to bed. It must have been about four o'clock when a slight noise somewhere in the house woke me. The sound seemed to come from downstairs. I listened, and hearing nothing further, I concluded it must have been my imagination.'

He paused and passed his tongue over his dry lips. 'I was preparing to go to sleep again when I heard a shout from down below, followed by a banging of a door. I rose and came downstairs to see what was the matter. Wills was standing by the front door, which he had just opened. He informed me that he had been disturbed by the sound of someone in my study, and very bravely had come down to investigate. He was in time to see the figure of a man, whom he says was dressed entirely in black, in the act of crossing the hall. Wills shouted, and the man rushed to the front door, pulled it open and slipped through, shutting the door behind him. Wills hurried to the door, but when he got there and looked out into the street the mysterious visitor was nowhere to be seen.'

'Was anything stolen?' asked Dick.

'That's the extraordinary part of it,' replied Mrs. Lathbury. His hands were becoming steadier, and he was assuming more and more of his usual pompous manner. 'Nothing was taken beyond an envelope from my safe, which contained only a number of private papers of no possible value to anyone but myself. It's a complete mystery — a complete mystery.'

'How did the man get in?' asked Dick. Mr. Lathbury shook his head.

'I have not the least idea,' he declared. 'I have not even had time to look. My first thought, directly I saw that horrible card on the desk, was to phone for you.'

Trent rose to his feet. 'Can I use your telephone?' he asked.

'Certainly,' said Lathbury, carefully hoisting his large body out of the chair and leading the way out into the hall. He indicated the instrument, which stood on a little table against the wall. Dick picked up the receiver and gave the number.

'Can I speak to Inspector Cowles?' he asked, when at length a sleepy voice answered him.

'He hasn't come in yet.'

'All right. Tell him it was Richard Trent, and ask him if he'll come along to Grosvenor Square at once.' He hung up the receiver and turned to the banker. 'I should like to see the study,' he said briefly.

Lathbury took him up the stairs onto the first landing. As they entered the big room Dick paused on the threshold, his eyes taking in at a glance every detail. The room was in the utmost disorder, the floor strewn and littered with papers. The big desk that stood in the centre had been forced open, the drawers pulled out and their contents emptied and scattered in every direction, and the drawers themselves piled up in a heap by the side. The safe that stood in one corner yawned wide open, its door hanging drunkenly on its hinges. One side of the carpet had been rolled back, disclosing the dark stained floor beneath. It was obvious that the mysterious intruder had been looking for something.

'You say an envelope was taken?' said Trent, turning to Lathbury. 'Are you sure that is all?'

The banker hesitated. 'I have not been able to ascertain whether there is anything else missing or not,' he replied. 'I thought it better to leave the place untouched until you arrived.'

Dick crossed over to the safe and surveyed the battered door. It was of the latest pattern advertised by its makers as burglar-proof, a fallacy that the ease with which it had been opened demonstrated.

'The man who smashed this knew his job,' said Trent. He stooped as he spoke and looked closer. 'He worked with rubber gloves, too, so there is no hope of finding fingerprints.'

He left the safe and went over to the desk. Lying on the top of the litter of papers was a white card the size of a visiting card. At the sight of the familiar black stamped impression on it, Trent's lips set in a firm line. 'I suppose you've no idea what the Hooded Terror could have been looking for?' he asked Lathbury.

'No,' answered the banker. 'I am completely puzzled.'

'What did the missing envelope contain?'

'Merely some private memoranda,' said Lathbury, 'connected with the bank. It was of no value — no value at all.'

'I think,' said Dick, 'you had better make certain that nothing else has been stolen while I speak to Wills.' Lathbury nodded and began to straighten out the collection of papers that littered the floor.

Dick found Wills in the hall, and led the perturbed butler into the dining room. 'Now, Wills,' he began, 'I want to ask you one or two questions. What was the noise that first woke you up?'

The old man thought for a moment before replying. 'I can't exactly say, sir,' he answered presently. 'It was nothing definite, just a vague sort of sound, a kind of crackling. I thought at first the master had possibly been taken ill. He mentioned that he wasn't feeling very well when he came in. I thought I'd come down and see if I could do anything.' He stopped.

'What happened next?' prompted Dick.

'I slipped on a coat,' continued the old butler, 'and opened the door of my room, which is at the top of the house, and I came down the stairs. When I got onto the landing, the one above that which the study opens onto, I heard the sound of rustling papers. As I came down the next flight of stairs I saw that there was a light in the study, the door was partly open, and it was from there that the sound came.

'I was halfway down the stairs when the door opened wide, and a man came out. Though I could not see his face, for it was too dark, I knew it was not the master. He was much taller and thinner. I shouted, and the man was startled and made a rush for the front door. I ran after him, but he was too quick for me. Before I could get near he had pulled open the door and run through, banging it behind him. I opened it, hoping to get a glimpse of him in the street outside, but there was no sign of him; and at that moment Mr. Lathbury appeared, asking what had happened.'

'You have no idea who the man was?' asked Trent.

The old butler shook his head slowly. 'I never saw his face,' he replied, 'but he was dressed entirely in black, and wore a soft hat pulled low over his eyes.'

'You usually see to the locking up before going to bed?' asked Dick.

'Yes, sir,' said Wills.

'And how is the front door fastened?'

'Bolted and chained,' replied the old man.

'Was this done last night?'

'Yes, sir.'

'And the man would not have had time to unbolt and unchain the door before he left?'

'He didn't, sir,' replied the butler. 'He just pulled it open.'

'Humph!' said Dick thoughtfully. 'He must have prepared his means of exit beforehand. You heard no other sound,' he continued, 'but the noise that woke you?'

'No, sir,' replied Wills. 'Nothing.'

'Take me through to the back,' said Trent. 'I want to find out how the man got in.'

The butler led the way across the hall to a door at the far end, which led down a short flight of steps into the kitchen. Crossing this, he unbolted and unchained a small half-glass door covered with iron shutters, which led into the garden.

Dick had not to look far to discover the means by which the intruder had gained an entrance. Reared against one side of the house was a light ladder, the top resting against an upper windowsill. He turned to the old man at his side and pointed upwards. 'What window is that?' he asked.

'The bathroom, sir,' replied Wills.

Dick approached the ladder; and as he came near the foot where it rested on the gravel, his eyes caught sight of something white that showed up faintly in the darkness, lying close by. Stooping, he picked it up. It was a handkerchief, a tiny thing of silk and lace. Returning to the kitchen, he switched on the light and examined his find. It was a woman's handkerchief, and neatly embroidered in one corner were the initials C. B.

Dick slipped it into his pocket, his

mind in a whirl, for he knew the owner of that handkerchief. Unless he was very much mistaken it belonged to Christine Baker, James Lathbury's secretary!

6

Concerning an Overdraft

It was one of Richard Trent's boasts that he had outgrown sentiment, and that his interest in women was detached and purely of a philosophical nature. Yet the discovery of that tiny handkerchief caused him considerable worry concerning its owner. There was no possible doubt of its having belonged to Christine, for beside the initials it was redolent of the peculiar perfume she was in the habit of using.

But how in the world had it come to be at the foot of the ladder used by the intruder to break into Lathbury's residence? The most obvious answer seemed to be that it had been dropped by the girl, which proved that she must have been there at the time, even if she were not actually the person responsible for the robbery.

Dick had only seen her some half-dozen times, and had resolutely refused to allow himself to analyze his feelings concerning her. But in some inexplicable manner the girl had a habit of intruding herself upon his thoughts at odd moments in a way that was most disconcerting for a man who considered himself a confirmed bachelor.

After his discovery of the handkerchief, Dick tried once more to get through to Cowles, but the inspector was still out. After completing his formal inquiries, he phoned an account of the affair through to headquarters.

Shortly after this, an inspector arrived. Leaving him in charge, Dick, refusing Lathbury's offer of breakfast, set off for Scotland Yard. The rain of the previous night had ceased, and the morning was bright and clear. A faint pink tinge in the east heralded the appearance of the sun, and the air was clean and sweet. Dick elected to walk; for the deserted streets, soon to be filled with the roar and bustle of the day, were quiet and peaceful and conducive to thought, and Dick had quite a lot to occupy his mind. He felt hot-eyed and weary from lack of sleep, but after he had been walking for a little while the cool air acted like a tonic and soon banished his feeling of fatigue.

He had left James Lathbury bordering on collapse, for the robbery seemed to have reduced the stout banker to a state almost akin to terror. What possible motive could the Hooded Terror have had for the burglary? mused Dick as he turned into Oxford Street. Apparently the only thing stolen had been the envelope, which, according to the banker, contained nothing of value. Lathbury had carefully examined his other papers and effects, and had announced that nothing else was missing.

It was inconceivable that the Hooded Terror had broken in on the off-chance of finding a large sum of money in the safe. It was quite unlike his usual method, for every outrage in which he had been concerned had been carefully planned down to the minutest detail, in advance, and he never undertook a job that was not certain to yield a considerable profit.

That he should have taken the risk of breaking into Lathbury's house for the sake of an envelope containing a few papers relating to the business of the bank was absurd, unless —

Dick stopped suddenly in his walk, and a constable standing at the corner of a side street eyed him suspiciously.

With startling suddenness, an idea had flashed through his mind. An idea vague and shadowy, true, but certainly full of possibilities. He was still turning this new theory over in his mind when he arrived at Scotland Yard and turned in through the Whitehall entrance.

It was barely six a.m., and the sergeant on duty in the entrance looked at him in surprise as he crossed to the stone steps leading up to his office. 'You're early, sir,' the man remarked with a smile.

'I've given up sleeping,' answered Dick cheerfully, and ascended the stairs.

When he reached his room he rang and ordered some hot coffee, then sat down at his desk to think. For some time he sat and stared before him with unseeing eyes, his alert mind grappling with the nebulous idea that had taken shape in his brain.

Presently he picked up the telephone and gave a number. After a few minutes he was in communication with Lathbury. 'Can you tell me exactly what that envelope contained that was stolen?' Dick enquired.

There was a pause at the other end of the wire. 'Well, er — er,' came the hesitant voice of Mr. Lathbury, 'the contents were some papers relating to — er — a private matter concerning one of my clients at the bank. I am by no means sure that I am within my — er — rights in — er — divulging their nature.'

There was another pause, and Dick waited patiently.

'Under the circumstances, however,' continued the banker, 'I suppose it is necessary that you should know — provided, of course, that you treat the matter confidentially. I see no reason — no reason at all why I should not inform you.'

Dick made a grimace at the telephone

as the slow, pompous voice proceeded.

'As a matter of fact, they were concerning an overdraft, and I had brought them home the day before yesterday to work on — I sometimes do part of my business at home in the evenings. They merely consisted of a list of securities offered, and ideally were of no value to anybody.'

'What was the name of the person who required the overdraft?' asked Dick.

Mr. Lathbury was so long in replying that Dick thought he had rung off, but presently his voice sounded again, slowly and reluctantly. 'Morrison,' he replied. 'Jack Morrison!'

Dick Trent was so astonished that he almost dropped the receiver; and as it was, he put it back on its hook without saying goodbye to Lathbury, or putting the further questions he had intended to ask.

Morrison! It was the last name that Dick had expected to hear, and it shattered his theory completely. There was no particular reason why he should feel astonished at the fact of Jack

Morrison trying to arrange an overdraft at his bank, beyond the fact he knew that Morrison had a considerable balance at the City and County; for it was only two days previously that he had mentioned to Dick, with great delight, some shares he had held that had suddenly boomed, rising in leaps and bounds. Morrison had sold out at the height of their value, and had netted something like twenty thousand pounds over the transaction. Of course, it might be a different Morrison altogether, and the similarity in names only a coincidence.

To make sure, Dick rang up Lathbury again. At the end of his enquiries there could be no possible doubt about it being the same Morrison, for Lathbury stated that his client was engaged on the staff of the *Monitor*, and there was certainly only one Morrison working for that enterprising paper.

As he sipped at the steaming coffee brought in by a constable, Dick tried to puzzle it out. What possible interest could a list of securities, offered by his friend in connection with an overdraft at the

Western and Union Bank, have for the Hooded Terror? And how did that mysterious individual know that the list was at Lathbury's house? It was only by chance that it was there, as ordinarily it would have been far more likely to have been kept at the bank.

Dick's heart sank as the obvious solution flashed to his mind — the handkerchief. Christine Baker was Lathbury's secretary, and her handkerchief was found at the bottom of the ladder by which the intruder had made his entrance. She, of course, would have been able to find out quite easily that the banker was taking the list home to work on. That led to only one conclusion: that she was in communication with the Hooded Terror!

Dick helped himself to a cigarette from the box on his desk and savagely struck a match. The whole thing was impossible, and made his head ache. With an exclamation that was more forcible than polite, he rose to his feet, jammed his hands in his pocket, and started to pace up and down the room.

He was conscious of an almost overpowering desire to see Christine, and turned to the telephone directory before he realized that in all probability she was not on the phone; and in any case, it was foolishness to put a call through at that hour.

He closed the book he had half-opened with a bang, and turned as a tap came at the door. Inspector Cowles entered, beautifully dressed as usual, but looking pale and haggard.

'Hello, Cowles,' greeted Dick. 'I've phoned you twice at your flat, but they said you hadn't been home. Where have you been?'

'They told me you'd phoned — that's why I'm here,' said Cowles, sitting on the edge of the desk and swinging a perfectly trousered leg. 'Otherwise, I was going to have a short rest.' He yawned.

'Where the devil have you been?' asked Dick again.

Cowles grinned and searched for his cigarette case. 'I've been trailing an old friend of ours,' he announced, lighting a cigarette and blowing a cloud of blue smoke ceiling-wards.

'Who?' asked Dick.

'Sparkler Wallace,' answered Cowles. 'I saw him at Victoria Station quite by chance, and during our brief conversation he hinted rather broadly that someone was out to get me. In fact, he seemed to know so much that I decided it was worthwhile following him. I'm glad I did, for I've learned a lot.'

'Well, while you've been chasing after Wallace, things have been happening,' said Dick. 'The Hooded Terror got busy again. Lathbury's house was broken into last night.'

'I know,' replied Inspector Cowles calmly, flicking the ash from his cigarette daintily with his little finger.

Dick stopped dead in his pacing and stared at his colleague. 'You know! How the deuce do you know?' he demanded.

'I was there!' said the inspector. 'I'll tell you who did the job. It was Sparkler Wallace!'

'Do you mean that Wallace is the Hooded Terror?' Dick almost shouted.

Detective Inspector Cowles shook his

head. 'No,' he answered. 'I believe he's one of the gang, but I don't think he's the big noise. I'm hoping he'll lead us to him, though. I'll tell you all about it, and you can judge for yourself. There are several things I don't understand. The girl's one of them.'

'What girl?' asked Dick with a sudden tightening of his heart, as he remembered the handkerchief which reposed in his breast pocket.

'Oh, there's a girl in it,' said Cowles, staring at the highly polished toe cap of his patent shoe. 'How she fits in I don't know, but she's in it somewhere. I thought it was the fair Lydia at first, but it wasn't.'

He took a long pull at his cigarette. 'Wallace's remarks at the station,' he continued after a short silence, 'made me think, and I was convinced that he knew something about this Hooded Terror business. I trailed him when he left, and shortly afterward he met his wife — you remember Lydia, don't you? As usual they played the same old trick, pretending to be entire strangers, and took separate first-class tickets. I took a ticket to the same destination — the booking clerk gave me the information when I let him know who I was — but I travelled third. I'd have given a lot to have been able to hear what they were talking about, but of course it was impossible.

'About twelve miles down the line they got out. The little station was almost deserted, and it took me all my time to avoid being spotted. They still pretended they didn't know each other, and crossed over the bridge to the 'up' platform. In about fifteen minutes a train came in and Wallace and Lydia got into a first-class carriage. I waited in the shadow of the bridge steps until they were safely inside, and then, just as the train was moving off, I sprinted for it and managed to scramble in the end carriage.

'Up to now things had been pretty dull, and I was beginning to get a bit bored. We were obviously bound for Victoria again, unless they intended getting out at one of the intervening stations, which I thought was unlikely. However, I was hoping that something would happen when we got back — and it did!

'When we drew up at Victoria, Lydia was the first out of the train, and scurried off up the platform as hard as she could go. I wasn't a bit interested in her. I knew where to find her if I wanted her; it was Wallace I was after.'

Cowles scrunched out the stub of his cigarette in the ashtray and lit another. 'I thought possibly,' he went on, 'that having left his wife he might do something, or go somewhere, that would give me a line to the Terror. It was fairly certain that there was something in the wind. Wallace and Lydia never meet unless there's something big afoot.

'He strolled quite leisurely out of the station and hailed a taxi in Victoria Street. I followed in another. Wallace got out at the entrance to a big block of flats — Camberly Mansions in Maida Vale — paid off the driver, and went in. This looked like a tame ending to the evening's amusement, for it seemed as if Wallace had merely gone home to bed. However, having gone so far I thought I might as well hang about a bit longer, in case anything happened.

'The lamp in the entrance hall was still alight, and I saw him enter a flat on the ground floor. The windows overlook the street; and just after he had entered, a light appeared in the windows of his flat. It was impossible to see into the room, for the window was covered by heavy draw-curtains. Near the bottom, however, these had not quite met, and I determined to try and get a glimpse inside. From the main pathway that leads to the entrance, a narrow band of grass encircles the entire block — you know how I mean?'

Dick nodded. He was intensely interested in Cowles's recital of his night's adventures.

'It was past twelve, and the road was quite deserted,' continued the immaculate detective inspector, brushing the leg of his trousers with his handkerchief where some ash had fallen from his cigarette, 'so I decided to take a peep through those curtains. It was evidently Wallace's sitting room. I must say, that fellow's got great ideas on making himself comfortable. He had taken off his coat, and was in his shirt sleeves; and what do you think he was doing?'

Dick shook his head, and Cowles chuckled softly.

'He was engaged in examining a limp leather hold-all. It was one of the neatest and most perfect outfits of burglar's tools that I've seen. Directly I saw that, I knew that my evening had not been wasted. After he had carefully looked them through, he rolled up the hold-all, put it in his pocket, and left the room, switching out the light.

'As there was nothing more to see, I returned to the street. It was one of the longest vigils I've ever kept, and I can tell you I began to get jolly cold. After two hours had gone by, and nothing further happened, I felt sure that I had made a mistake. I had just arrived at this decision, when out came Wallace. He had changed, and was dressed entirely in black.

'I hadn't the least idea where he was going, but he set off at a good pace towards the West End. It's a long walk from Maida Vale to Grosvenor Square, but I think we must have done it in something like record time. I was never more surprised in my life when I found out Wallace's destination. He slowed up outside Lathbury's house. I knew the place, because I'd been there before, in connection with the robbery at the Western and Union Bank. There's a narrow opening that runs down the side of the house, a sort of mews, and Sparkler, after looking about, made for this and disappeared down it. I went after him, and was just in time to see him climb over a wall at the end into the banker's garden.

'I wondered for a moment whether I should follow him, or wait for him to come out. Of course, I could have arrested him at once, but that wouldn't have suited my plans. I wanted to find out what his game was.

'I'd just made up my mind to go after him when I heard the sound of someone climbing back over the wall. I thought it was friend Wallace returning, and crouched down in the shadows in case he should spot me. But it wasn't Wallace. It was a girl!

'The girl dropped over the wall,' continued Cowles, 'and sped up the alley like the wind. I was so astonished that I let her go, and by the time I'd recovered and run to the top of the passage, she'd vanished, and there was no sign of her. I haven't the faintest idea who she was. She was much too tall for Lydia.'

'You didn't see her face?' asked Dick.

'It was too dark,' replied Cowles, 'but I should know her again if I came across her.'

'How?' rapped out Dick quickly.

'As she ran by me I smelt a whiff of perfume. It was a peculiar perfume. I smelt it once before somewhere, but I can't remember where.'

Dick could have told him, but he didn't. He had decided to keep the finding of Christine's handkerchief to himself. 'What happened next?' he asked, to change the subject.

'Well,' continued Cowles, 'having lost the girl, I waited to see what had happened to Wallace. I waited for about twenty minutes. Suddenly the front door opened with a bang. He came tearing down the steps and made off as hard as he could go in the direction of Oxford Street.

'I went after him, and was just in time to see him pick up a belated taxi. There wasn't another in sight, so I couldn't follow him, but I guessed he had gone home. To make sure, I went back to Camberly Mansions — and I was right, for the windows of his flat were lighted. I waited about a bit to make sure he wasn't coming out again. Very soon the light went out, and I concluded he had gone to bed, so I decided to go home. When I got to my flat, I found you had rung up twice, so I changed and came on here.'

Cowles paused for a moment. 'What I want to know is, what did he break into old Lathbury's for?' he continued musingly, stroking his smoothly brushed hair with the palm of his hand.

'I can tell you that,' said Dick, 'but it doesn't help us much. In fact, it only adds to the mystery. All that was stolen was an envelope containing a list of securities belonging to a client of Lathbury's, and relating to an overdraft at the bank.'

'The securities themselves weren't there?' asked Cowles.

'No,' replied Dick, shaking his head, 'only a list. And if you can tell me why Wallace should go to the trouble of breaking into Lathbury's house to secure something that was of absolutely no value at all, you're cleverer than I am.'

Cowles scratched his chin thoughtfully. 'Who was the overdraft for?' he asked.

'You'll never guess in a thousand years,' said Dick. 'Jack Morrison.'

'Last Minute Morrison?' he inquired. Dick nodded. 'I didn't know he had an account at Lathbury's bank,' said Cowles.

'Neither did I,' answered Dick. 'I always thought his account was at the City and County. Anyway, what he wanted an overdraft for beats me, because I know he's got a fairly big balance there.'

'Do you mean to say,' said Cowles, 'that Wallace went to all that trouble merely for the sake of a list of securities?'

'It does seem queer, doesn't it?' said Dick. 'But old Lathbury went through all his effects, and there was nothing else stolen. Anyway, you were quite right in thinking that Wallace is in some way connected with the Hooded Terror, because the man who burgled Lathbury left one of those confounded cards on the desk.'

'I am sure Wallace is not the Terror himself,' said Cowles, 'although I believe he is one of the gang.'

'Why didn't you pull him in at once after the robbery?' asked Dick.

'Because,' said Cowles, 'we're after the big fish, and I'm hoping Wallace will lead us to him. Once we get the central figure, the others will take care of themselves.' He paused and added, 'I should like to know what part that girl played in the matter, and who she was.'

Dick didn't answer. Cowles, noticing his unaccustomed silence, shot a peculiar glance at him.

'The robbery has upset old Lathbury completely,' said Dick, after a pause. Cowles noted the quick way in which he had again changed the subject. 'He seems to have gone all to pieces; anybody would think he had lost a fortune.'

'I suppose,' said Cowles, 'he is speaking the truth, and the envelope was the only thing stolen?'

'That's what he says,' replied Dick. 'And I don't see why he should lie about it if he had lost anything else. You mustn't forget that this is the second time the Hooded Terror has singled Lathbury out for a victim.'

'I know,' said Cowles. 'It's curious, isn't it?'

He thrust his hands deeply into his trouser pockets, and for a few moments neither spoke. It was Cowles who at length broke the silence. 'Dick,' he said, seriously, 'I would give a few years of my life to lay my hands on the Terror. I have considered every criminal known to the police, and rejected them all. There is only one man I can think of who possessed sufficient brains to make a success of an organization like the Hooded Terror gang, and he is dead; so it can't be him.'

'You mean Hammer Stevens,' said Dick, smiling.

'Yes,' said Cowles. 'It's a funny thing that whenever I think of the Hooded Terror, I always think of Stevens. If he was alive I shouldn't bother to look any further.'

'I don't think the Terror has ever been known to the police,' said Dick. 'And he works alone — that is to say, his gang are mere puppets, he knows them all but they don't know him; and that is why he is safe. Not one of his organization know his real identity, and could not give him away if they wanted to.'

'Except Blackie Phrynne,' said Cowles grimly.

'His knowledge wasn't much use to him,' said Dick. 'The Hooded Terror — '

At that moment there came a rap at the door and a constable entered. 'There's a gentleman wants to see you, sir,' he said to Dick.

'What's his name?' asked Dick.

'Mr. Morrison of the *Monitor*,' replied the policeman.

'Oh, show him in,' said Dick. 'I suppose he has come about the Lathbury affair,' he added, turning to Cowles. The inspector nodded.

A moment later Jack Morrison entered the office. 'Hello, you two!' he greeted them jovially. 'You're early this morning. Strange business at Lathbury's. I have just been round there. More of the Hooded Terror's work, eh? I've got most of the particulars, but I was wondering if you would give me anything else.'

'I expect you know almost as much as we do,' answered Dick. 'You're pretty good at nosing out information, and if you have seen Lathbury, I don't suppose there's much left for me to tell you.'

Morrison chuckled. 'Lathbury's in an awful funk,' he said. 'He looks ghastly. When I left him he was talking of going to bed and sending for a doctor. Said he didn't feel capable of going to the bank today.'

'By the way,' said Dick suddenly, 'I never knew you had an account at Lathbury's bank, Jack.'

Morrison looked up at him quickly. 'It's quite a small one,' he replied. 'How did you know?'

Dick answered him with a question.

'Did Lathbury tell you what was stolen?' he asked.

Morrison nodded.

'Yes,' he replied, 'an envelope containing some memoranda relating to a client of his at the bank.'

'He didn't tell you the name of the client?' asked Dick.

'No,' answered Morrison. 'He said the contents of the envelope were of no value. I thought it queer that the Hooded Terror should have gone to all that trouble for nothing, but he didn't tell me who they related to.'

'Well, they concerned you,' said Dick quietly.

Morrison's face was a picture of astonishment. 'Me!' he repeated incredulously.

'Yes,' said Dick. 'They were a list of securities which you had given Lathbury, relating to an overdraft.'

The star reporter of the *Monitor* was silent for several moments. 'It is perfectly true, I was arranging an overdraft,' he said at last, 'on the security of some shares, the description of which I left with

Lathbury a few days ago. I can't for the life of me see what interest the Hooded Terror could have in those.'

'What did you want the overdraft for, Jack?' asked Dick. 'I thought you had quite a big balance at the City and County.'

For a moment Morrison looked confused. 'It was a matter of business,' he replied vaguely. 'I have to find quite a large sum of money during the next few days. It is quite a private matter, and could not help you at all.' He looked at his watch. 'If you can't give me any other information about the affair, I'll be getting along to the office. I want to get my copy in early. Goodbye, Cowles.'

He was halfway to the door when Dick stopped him. 'If you're not busy tonight, Jack,' he said, resting a hand on his shoulder, 'you might come and have a bit of food with me. I'd like to have a chat with you.'

'I have got a lot of work to get through,' replied Morrison. 'If I can get it done in time, I'll come along. At the flat, I suppose?'

Dick nodded absently. He had scarcely heard him, for his hand resting on Morrison's shoulder had come in contact with something hard, and he was wondering why Last Minute Morrison wore a bullet-proof waistcoat!

7

Mr. Stepping Receives a Visitor

Mr. Stepping awoke with a feeling of intense satisfaction. His night's work had been more successful than he had expected, and as he rose and set about preparing for his bath, he whistled cheerfully the strains of one of the latest foxtrots. Having dressed and prepared his breakfast (for Mr. Stepping, for several reasons, did not keep a servant), he sat down to his solitary meal with a good appetite.

His thoughts were pleasant ones, for locked in a small safe in his bedroom was an envelope the contents of which, he considered, properly handled, were equivalent to a fortune. He had taken a considerable risk to obtain it, but the result had been far above anything he had expected. He chuckled softly to himself as he poured out a second cup of tea, and, having finished his breakfast, lighted a cigarette.

It was past eleven, for Mr. Stepping had lost a considerable amount of sleep on the previous night, and had made up for it by rising late. Having finished his tea, he rose to his feet, and entering the bedroom, crossed over to the small safe that stood in one corner. Unlocking this, he withdrew a long envelope and returned with it to the dining room. For over half an hour he examined the contents. Then, making his way to the telephone which stood on a little table beside the bed, he took the receiver from its hook and called a number. His conversation lasted for ten minutes, and the man at the other end, who had been listening, replaced the receiver with a shaking hand and wiped the perspiration from his forehead. For in that ten minutes Mr. Stepping had pronounced the other's doom, and left the fear of death in his eyes.

For the rest of the day Mr. Stepping did nothing; that is to say, he did nothing of any consequence. Armed with a book, he settled himself comfortably on the sofa in his sitting room, syphon and decanter at his elbow, and read and smoked the hours away, only stirring once to prepare himself a frugal lunch which, owing to the lateness of his breakfast, he partook of about four o'clock in the afternoon. Having satisfied his hunger, he returned to the sofa and his book.

In the gentle and difficult art of doing nothing gracefully, Mr. Harold Stepping — or, to give him his correct name, Wallace — was a past master; and the day went by, as far as he was concerned, pleasantly enough. He felt at peace with the world, for he imagined that he was on the verge of pulling off the coup of his life. And it seemed so easy, far easier than anything he had ever attempted before.

Dusk was falling when there suddenly came a gentle tap on the front door of the flat, and with a smile Stepping laid aside the book he had been reading and rose. Passing along the short corridor, he opened the door softly. There was no light in the hall. Against the blue square of the fading day a figure loomed up duskily.

'I thought you'd come, Steve,' remarked Mr. Stepping genially, and closed the door carefully behind his visitor as soon as he had stepped across the threshold.

*   *   *

Soon after Last Minute Morrison had left Dick's office at Scotland Yard, Inspector Cowles also took his departure, with the avowed intention of snatching a few hours' rest to try and make up for the amount he had lost on the previous night.

Left to himself, Dick paced up and down the big room, trying to grapple with the problem that was weighing on his mind. His conscience was beginning to trouble him at having kept the finding of the handkerchief a secret from Cowles. Not that he regretted his action in any way; but in view of his position, it was a serious matter to have suppressed a clue which was certainly of inestimable value in running to earth the perpetrator of the robbery.

What had Christine been doing at Lathbury's house in the middle of the

89

night? Although he tried to find a solution to this in every conceivable way, Dick could not think of one which appeared to him to be at all possible. Reason seemed to indicate clearly that the girl was in some way connected with the Hooded Terror, but in his heart of hearts Dick could not believe it. There must be some other explanation to account for her presence in Lathbury's garden. There was no direct evidence to show that she had entered the house, and equally there was no evidence to show that she had not.

It took him some time to come to a decision, but at last, after he had worried himself over the matter for the best part of an hour, he made up his mind to go down to the bank and catch the girl as she came out to lunch. Perhaps if he questioned her, he thought, he might be able to learn something that would clear the matter up. Probably she would be able to explain away the handkerchief.

On his way towards the city, his mind reverted to the discovery he had made that morning of the fact that Jack Morrison was in the habit of wearing a bullet-proof waistcoat, and he wondered what in the world his reason could be. It was certainly unusual for a newspaper reporter to take such a precaution, unless it was that since Morrison had joined in the chase of the Hooded Terror he was (remembering the attempt on Cowles) becoming cautious and taking no risks of having his career suddenly cut short by an unseen bullet.

Dick arrived at the Western and Union Bank a full half-hour too early, and proceeded to walk up and down on the opposite side of the road to the entrance, filling in his time by running over the story Cowles had told him of his adventure on the previous night. Thus occupied, the half-hour passed fairly quickly; so quickly, in fact, that it was with a start of surprise that Dick suddenly espied the slim figure of Christine Baker descending the steps of the bank. She looked radiantly pretty and greeted Dick with a smile as he hurried across the road to meet her.

'This is a surprise, Mr. Trent,' she declared, holding out a small gloved hand. Dick felt suddenly elated as he detected the note of pleasure in her voice. 'What are you doing in this part of the world?'

'Until a moment ago,' he replied, 'I was waiting for you.'

'For me?' she repeated.

'Yes,' he answered gaily, walking along by her side. 'I got thoroughly tired of the environments of Scotland Yard, and conceived a sudden and violent antipathy for anything that remotely resembled a policeman, so I decided to come and see if I could persuade you to let me take you out to lunch.'

'It is very nice of you,' she replied, 'and I don't think I shall need much persuading. It will certainly prove a new experience, as far as I'm concerned.'

'Why, what do you mean?' he asked curiously.

'Well, it will be the first time I've ever lunched with a detective,' she replied, laughing. 'I begin to feel already as if I were under arrest.'

'I can assure you,' remarked Dick, 'it's not the usual habit for detectives to provide their prisoners with lunch.'

He led the way down a little side street towards a restaurant. The place at that hour was fairly crowded, but Dick managed to find a vacant table in one corner, and to this he escorted his pretty companion. Many envious eyes followed him as he crossed the room, for Christine was a girl who possessed that type of beauty which even women look at twice.

She stripped off her gloves while Dick consulted the menu and gave their order. 'I shan't be able to stay very long,' she said, 'as we're very busy today. Mr. Lathbury hasn't turned up, which makes my work all the harder.'

'I suppose he hasn't recovered from last night yet,' said Dick.

'It was a dreadful affair, wasn't it?' said the girl. 'What could have been the reason for the robbery? We didn't hear much about it at the bank, except what Mr. Lathbury told the chief cashier when he phoned up this morning to say that he wouldn't be coming today; but I heard that nothing was stolen. Is that true?'

'Nothing of any importance,' said Dick

cautiously. 'The whole thing was mysterious, but then everything connected with the Hooded Terror is mysterious.'

As he mentioned the name of the elusive criminal, a slight shadow seemed to pass across the girl's face, and in her blue eyes there shone for a moment the faintest trace of an expression of fear. Dick, who was looking steadily at her at the moment, noticed it, but it was gone in a flash, and the next instant the girl was herself again.

'Have you found out anything fresh?' she asked after a slight pause. 'Anything likely to lead to the discovery of his real identity?'

Dick shook his head. 'No,' he replied. 'Sometimes I almost begin to believe that we never shall. It's like looking for a person in a fog. Every now and again you think you've got them, and then you find that what you thought was solid turns out to be only a shadow after all.'

He waited while the waitress set the soup before them. 'Now and again there springs up a really clever criminal,' he continued when the girl had gone. 'A genius who doesn't make mistakes, and the Hooded Terror seems to be one of these. Perhaps one of these days he'll make a slip. That's all we can hope for.'

'He won't!' she answered almost absently, and then flushed crimson as she realized what she had said. 'I mean,' she added quickly, 'from what I have heard of the Hooded Terror, he's too clever to do anything that's likely to leave a clue for the police.'

Dick looked at her quickly. 'What have you heard?' he asked.

She looked confused for a moment. 'Only what I've read in the papers,' she answered. 'And Mr. Lathbury has often discussed him. It's his favorite topic — I wish he'd keep to it,' she added irrelevantly.

'Why?' inquired Dick astonished.

'Well,' she answered, 'it would keep him off subjects that — that — ' She hesitated. ' — that are less unpleasant,' she ended lamely, and catching Dick's eye she flushed.

Suddenly he understood her meaning. 'Has that — that old jellyfish been making advances to you?' he demanded heatedly; and then, 'I beg your pardon. I had no right to ask you that.'

'It's quite all right,' she answered, smiling. 'To be perfectly candid, he has not only been making advances to me, but he has asked me to marry him.'

'He must be mad,' exclaimed Dick wrathfully.

'That's hardly complimentary, is it?' she murmured, laughing outright.

'I-I didn't mean it like that,' stammered Dick. 'I meant a man of his age — it's preposterous!'

He was so vehement that she was secretly amused. 'Of course I shall have to leave if he persists,' she said. 'But I'm used to the work. And just now, when Mr. Lathbury appears so ill and upset, it would hardly be fair to go and give him all the trouble of having to initiate a stranger into the job. And after all, he's always treated me decently.'

They chatted on, and Dick was deriving so much pleasure at merely being with the girl that they were halfway through lunch before he remembered, with a pang, his real object in seeking her out. He glanced at her as she toyed daintily with an omelet, and suppressed a sigh. This girl with the flawless features and gentle voice, whom he had met but half a dozen times in his life, was beginning to mean more to him than he cared to admit, even to himself. It was surely impossible that she could be in any way connected with a brutal murderer and thief. But how could the evidence against her be explained away?

She noticed his preoccupation and looked curiously at him, wondering what it was that had suddenly made him so silent. She liked this clear-eyed, clean-limbed young man, and was unaccountably attracted by his personality. He was in some peculiar way different from the few men of his own age that she had met. He seemed more solid, more reliable. She felt that in a crisis he was the kind of man one would instantly turn to, and be certain of not making a mistake.

He raised his eyes and caught her looking at him. She blushed and glanced down at her plate. The task he had set himself had to be accomplished, and he cast round in his mind for an opening. It was Christine herself who supplied him with one. Picking up her handbag, she searched about in its interior, and uttered a little exclamation of annoyance.

'What's the matter?' he asked.

'I've lost my handkerchief,' she replied, 'or else I've stupidly come out without one. It doesn't really matter.'

With a quickening of his pulse, Dick slipped his hand into his breast pocket and drew out the handkerchief he had found in Lathbury's garden. He laid it on the table in front of her. 'Is that one of yours?' he asked.

She looked at it wonderingly. 'Yes,' she answered, picking it up and examining the initials in the corner. 'Where did you get it?'

He looked at her steadily as he replied, 'I found it in James Lathbury's garden just after the burglary.'

The colour receded from her face, leaving it deathly white. 'I-I don't understand,' she murmured in a voice that trembled slightly.

'It was lying at the bottom of the ladder the intruder had used to reach the upper window by which he got in,' explained Dick. 'How did it come there?'

He saw her start and tremble; saw the tremendous effort with which she tried to recover her composure. 'I-I — How should I know?' she managed to stammer out at last.

'Miss Baker,' he answered, 'I am going to ask you a straight question. Please don't be annoyed. Were you at Lathbury's house last night?'

A tiny hint of defiance crept into the girl's eyes as she met his questioning glance, but she remained silent.

'I am not asking in an official capacity,' continued Dick, leaning forward earnestly. 'No one besides myself knows of the finding of this handkerchief. I want, if possible, to help you — as a friend.'

Her face was ashen, but her eyes softened slightly at his words. 'I'm afraid I can tell you nothing,' she said in a low voice after a pause.

'But you were there,' he persisted. 'You

were seen leaving the garden.'

'I-I was seen!' Her whisper was almost inaudible. 'Who saw me?'

'You were not recognized,' he answered gently, 'but that was because the person who saw you knew nothing about the handkerchief. Why don't you tell me the truth?' he urged. 'And let me help you. What part did you play in last night's robbery, and — '

'Oh, stop!' She flung out her hands in a gesture of appeal. 'I can't tell you. I can't!'

Dick felt a cold weight at his heart. Her fear and agitation could only be caused by one reason: that she possessed some guilty knowledge of the affair.

Her eyes were searching his face; and as she saw the doubt that began to creep into his expression, a little sob passed her white lips. 'I'd tell you if I could,' she breathed, 'but it's not my secret. All I can say is that I was not there for any wrong purpose. Won't you trust me?'

She looked at Dick appealingly and, as he read the pain and trouble in her eyes, his heart softened. He stretched out his hand and laid it on hers. Her hand was as cold as ice, and trembled, but she made no attempt to draw it away.

'I'll trust you,' he answered, and was rewarded by a faint smile that struggled desperately to break through unshed tears.

At the door of the bank he left her, after exacting a promise to let him take her to dinner one evening during the week, and made his way back to Scotland Yard.

Christine watched his tall figure until it was out of sight, and then instead of entering the bank, she made her way to the nearest call office and over the telephone poured out her story of the conversation into the sympathetic ears of the man who was listening at the other end of the wire.

8

A Telephone Message

Detective Inspector John Cowles, as immaculate as ever, and looking considerably fresher after his brief rest, sat at the desk in Richard Trent's room at Scotland Yard, his chin resting on one cupped hand, deep in thought. A cigarette smouldered between his fingers, and a little pile of crushed-out stubs filled the ashtray in front of him, testifying to the deepness of his cogitations. For when Cowles was engaged in trying to puzzle out a particularly knotty problem, he became a chain-smoker, lighting one cigarette from the butt of the other.

For a long time he sat thus, staring at the blotting pad; and then, apparently having suddenly arrived at some kind of decision, he stretched a long arm and pressed the bell. To the sergeant who presently entered in response to his summons, he gave an order. 'Go along to Records,' he said, 'and get me all that is known concerning Hammer Stevens, particulars of his convictions — everything, and any information they have concerning his death.'

The man departed, and after a long interval returned, bearing with him a pile of papers. Cowles spread them out on the desk and settled himself down to an enjoyable hour's quiet reading.

From a small bunch of photographs he selected one and studied it attentively. It was one of those sharp positives that police officials specialize in, and showed clearly whatever marks there were to be disclosed on the skin. The portrait was that of a young man, clean-shaven, and possessing a mop of unruly hair. At first glance the round, plump face seemed quite a pleasant one, until, looking closer, it was possible to discern a certain hardness about the eyes and a cruel little twist to the firm-set mouth that betrayed the man's real character. Beneath the photograph was written, 'Henry Stevens, D.M.'

The letters stood for the prison code. Every year was indicated by a capital letter of the alphabet. The D meant that he had suffered a term of imprisonment in Dartmoor. The M meant that he had been sentenced to another term.

Cowles read carefully the short but terrible record. The man had been convicted six times before he was twenty. The minor convictions were not designated by letters in the code. In a space at the foot of the card were the words, 'Dangerous, carries fire arms'; and in another hand, in red ink, was written, 'Killed during an attempt to escape from Dartmoor. Believed murdered by a man named Gordon Arkwright, who has since disappeared.'

He turned to another document to read the particulars of the dead man's crimes, and the comments of those who from time to time had been brought into official contact with him. In these scraps of information was contained the terrible history of the man. Even Cowles, hardened as he was to this kind of thing, was appalled as he read on.

Presently he came across a form headed, 'Description of Convicted Person'. Word by word he read it through: 'Henry Stevens, aka 'Hammer' Stevens, aka 'Knock-out' Steve.' There were two lines of different aliases. 'Height: 5ft. 6in. Chest: 38. Face: round. Complexion: fresh. Inclined to baldness.' This evidently was a later description, thought Cowles, than the photograph. 'Hair: brown. Speaks well, and writes good English. Excellent organizer, and possesses wonderful business capabilities. Favorite weapon: a leaden life preserver. As far as known, no relations. Specializes in bank robberies . . . ' There followed a list of measurements and body marks.

Cowles tucked up the papers and put them together in an orderly pile, then he drew towards him a paper folder. On the outside was written in his own hand, 'Notes on the Arkwright case'. He opened the folder and read for the twentieth time the collection of press cuttings and typed sheets it contained. One in particular occupied his attention for a considerable time. It was a long newspaper account, and the scare headlines were splashed across three columns.

ESCAPED CONVICT MURDERED.
THE NOTORIOUS 'HAMMER'
STEVENS ESCAPES FROM
DARTMOOR PRISON DURING
STORM. KILLED BY FORMER
ASSOCIATE IN LONELY HOUSE.
(From our Special Correspondent.)

'During the terrible storm which raged over Devonshire last night, and lasted for nearly four hours, a daring escape took place from the convict prison at Princetown.

'The escaped man, Henry Stevens, known to the police as 'Hammer' Stevens (and various other aliases), on account of his favorite method of bludgeoning his victims, was, it will be remembered, serving a life sentence for the attempted murder of the manager of the Trans-Atlantic Bank, in connection with the robbery which took place there nearly two years ago.'

Here followed an account of the robbery, which Cowles skipped.

'From the evidence of the prison officials, it appears that Stevens succeeded, in some ingenious way, in carrying into the prison without being detected, a heavy piece of stone from the quarries in which he had been working during the day. This he secreted in his cell and attacked the warder, who brought him his supper, and, while the man was unconscious, removed his uniform and dressed himself in it. In this guise, he managed to get to the exercise yard and made his escape by climbing the wall at a point where some repairs were in the process of being carried out.

'There was a special guard at this place, but it is believed that under cover of the noise made by the storm, Stevens managed to creep upon him and take him unawares, striking him down with the handle of a pick, which he took from a heap of tools which were lying near and were being used for the work on the wall. The guard states that he heard nothing prior to the blow, which rendered him senseless. It was not until he had recovered consciousness, some three-quarters of an hour later, and given the alarm, that the escape was discovered.

'Search parties of armed warders were immediately sent out in pursuit of Stevens, and all houses and villages nearby were warned, and the moor thoroughly combed for traces of the wanted man, but no sign of Stevens was found . . .'

Cowles missed half a column and went on from the foot of the page.

'On the edge of Dartmoor, occupying a particularly lonely position five miles from the prison and at least a mile from any other habitation, is a small farm occupied by a man named Arkwright, and one of the warders. Hardy, by name, suddenly remembered that this man, Arkwright, had been a friend of Stevens before his imprisonment. He mentioned this to two of his comrades, and they immediately set off to Arkwright's farm. The place is a low, long, rambling building in a very bad state of repair, and, since Arkwright's tenancy, has been neglected and uncared for. On approaching the farm the warders were surprised to find that the front door was wide open. They investigated further, and in the narrow hall made their gruesome discovery.

'Lying near the door was the dead body of the escaped convict. 'Hammer' Stevens had been killed by a shotgun that had been fired at such close range that his face was practically shot away! The body was still dressed in the warder's uniform in which Stevens had made his escape.

'The weapon with which the crime had been committed was lying about two yards from the body further down the passage. The warders instantly communicated with the prison, and later the governor identified the dead man as that of the convict, 'Hammer' Stevens.'

Cowles paused in his reading and stared thoughtfully across at the opposite wall. Then he turned again to the desk and took another cutting from the folder; it started abruptly and was evidently the continuation of another column.

'At the inquest which was held yesterday on the body of the convict, 'Hammer'

Stevens, who escaped from Princetown Prison during the night of September 8, during the terrible storm, several fresh facts were elicited. It appears that Gordon Arkwright, the tenant of the farmhouse in which the dead man's body was discovered, had for some time been suspected of being a receiver of stolen goods, and had been under the observation of detectives from Scotland Yard. They, however, had never been able to discover sufficient evidence against him to warrant an arrest. It was known that he and Stevens were acquainted, and the dead convict was frequently seen in Arkwright's company prior to his connection with the robbery of the Trans-Atlantic Bank.

'It will be remembered that the proceeds of this robbery were never recovered, and no amount of cross-examination in the part of the prosecuting counsel during the trial could elicit from Stevens the place in which he had hidden them. The police theory of the murder is that Stevens, after the robbery, deposited the money stolen from the Trans-Atlantic Bank with Arkwright. The bulk of the stolen property was in notes, the numbers of which were known to the police, and their idea is that they had been given to Arkwright by Stevens for the former to dispose of, being afraid to take the risk of passing them himself. The police believe that Stevens, immediately after his escape from prison, knowing that Arkwright occupied the farm close at hand, made his way there with the intention of getting his share of the stolen money, and to persuade Arkwright to hide him until the hue and cry had died down. For some reason or other a quarrel arose between the two men (possibly Arkwright refused to part with any of the money). Then Stevens threatened him, and in self-defence Arkwright snatched up the shotgun and killed him. Afterward, in the first panic of fear, he fled to escape the consequences of his act.

'At the little country station of High Tor, which is about a mile and a half from the farm, Arkwright seems to have been fairly well known. The stationmaster, on being questioned by the police, admitted that a man answering to Arkwright's description had taken a ticket and traveled by the early morning train to Truro . . . '

Cowles pushed the papers wearily away from him, and rising to his feet walked over to the window and stared out at the river. His theory seemed an impossible one, and the more he tried to find evidence in its favor the more he found himself up against a dead end.

Hammer Stevens was undoubtedly dead; and being so, he could not be the Hooded Terror. And yet . . . Cowles shrugged his shoulders impatiently. In spite of the mass of evidence against his theory, he couldn't get it out of his mind. Ever since the Hooded Terror had first appeared to startle London with his audacious crimes, Cowles had, for some indefinable reason, connected him with Hammer Stevens. He had had these extraordinary hunches before, and in nearly every case they proved to be correct. But in this case it was no use going against solid fact, and the governor of the prison himself had identified the body.

He was still staring moodily out at the

Embankment, watching the gathering shadows settle over the river as dusk approached, when the door opened and Dick Trent entered the room.

Inspector Cowles turned and nodded. 'Did you enjoy your lunch?' he asked casually, with a slight twinkle in his eye, and Dick gasped. The inspector smiled as he noted his superior's look of astonishment. 'I've had a man trailing you ever since that affair on the Embankment,' he explained. 'I thought it was safer, but it wasn't worth mentioning.'

'Why?' said Dick. 'Do you think the Hooded Terror is going to use me as a target for his pistol practice in future?'

'I think it highly probable,' replied Cowles coolly. 'Have you noticed anything rather extraordinary lately?'

Dick thought for a moment and then shook his head. 'No, I don't think so,' he answered. 'What do you mean?'

'I mean that just recently the Hooded Terror's activities have, to a certain point, ceased,' said Cowles. 'He hasn't committed any big crime for some weeks — any crime that was likely to bring him in a profit, I mean. He doesn't usually descend to petty larceny.'

Dick looked at him curiously. 'What are you getting at?' he demanded.

'I'm getting at this,' replied Cowles, coming over from the window and seating himself in his favorite position on the corner of the desk. 'For some reason or other, the Hooded Terror's in a panic! Who or what he's afraid of, I don't know, and I can't guess. It may be that he's afraid of us, and thinks we know more than we do; but whatever it is, he's scared, and he's too busy thinking about himself to bother with any fresh outrages.'

Dick smiled a trifle skeptically. 'What makes you think so?' he asked.

Cowles made a little grimace. 'Just a hunch, but I think everything points to it,' he replied. 'You mark my words, Trent, there's something brewing. There's a sort of unnatural quiet just as there is before a thunderstorm. What's in the wind, I don't know, but it's something big, something else — ' He paused and leaned slightly towards Dick. 'Morrison's got something up his sleeve. What is it? He knows a lot

more than he wants us to think he knows.'
He stopped and lighted a cigarette.

'I wonder why he always wears a bullet-proof waistcoat and carries two guns,' Cowles added softly.

'When did you find that out?' asked Dick curiously. 'I only discovered it this morning.'

'I knew it the night poor Blackie Phrynne was killed,' said Cowles, blowing out a wreath of blue smoke ceiling-wards. 'When I was pushing past Morrison in the hall. He carries one of the guns strapped under his left arm, and the other in his left hip pocket. You can see the bulge they make if you look for it.'

Dick was silent. 'Do you believe that Morrison is connected with the Hooded Terror?' he asked presently.

Cowles looked at him steadily. 'Why not?' he said. 'We know very little about him, although he's a friend of yours. He landed from Canada fifteen years ago. Since that time he has worked his way up to the position of star reporter on the *Monitor,* but beyond that we know nothing.'

Dick made a little helpless gesture. 'If we begin suspecting everybody who wears a bullet-proof waistcoat or carries fire-arms,' he said, 'we might as well start with the assistant commissioner — he does both.'

'By suspecting everybody — ' began Cowles, and stopped as the telephone bell rang insistently.

Dick picked up the receiver. 'Hello?' he said.

A high-pitched, squeaky voice sounded over the wire. 'Is that Richard Trent?' it asked. Dick replied in the affirmative. 'This is a warning,' continued the voice. 'You are becoming troublesome. Leave Christine Baker alone! Otherwise I shall have to treat you as I treated Blackie Phrynne, and as I have just treated Sparkler Wallace.'

'Who are you? Who is that speaking?' demanded Dick.

'The Hooded Terror!' came the reply, and there was a click at the other end as the receiver was hung up.

9

At Camberly Mansions

'Good heavens!' exclaimed Inspector Cowles when Dick briefly related what had happened. 'The infernal audacity of the man is amazing. Do you think he was speaking the truth about Wallace?'

'I do,' snapped Dick, 'and we're going to Camberly Mansions as fast as a taxi can take us. The exchange says that the call was put through from there.'

Followed by Cowles, Dick strode to the door, and a few seconds later they were on the Embankment. Remembering his previous experience, Cowles kept a sharp look-out up and down the dark thoroughfare, but he could see nothing suspicious. Dick, however, allowed three taxis to pass him before he finally hailed a fourth and jumped in.

'What do you expect to find?' said Cowles as they rolled swiftly away in the direction of Maida Vale.

'A dead man!' replied Dick grimly. 'The Hooded Terror wasn't talking for the sake of hearing his own voice. He meant what he said, and for some reason or other he's killed Wallace.'

'I wonder why,' murmured the inspector softly.

'What's the good of wondering *why* at anything the Hooded Terror does?' said Dick irritably, and Cowles relapsed into silence, leaving Dick to his own thoughts.

It was quite dark when the taxi drew to a halt in front of Camberly Mansions. As Dick and Inspector Cowles sprang out, the latter pointed to the windows of the ground floor flat occupied by Sparkler Wallace. No light gleamed from behind the curtains, which they could see were only partially drawn.

'Either he's out, or . . . ' said Dick, leaving the sentence unfinished.

'He may be in another room,' said Cowles, though his voice held no conviction in its tone.

'We can soon see,' answered Dick shortly, as he strode into the entrance.

At the front door, which faced the main door of the vestibule, he paused and listened at the flap of the letterbox. From within he could hear the sound of a clock ticking, but that was all; otherwise, the place was as silent as the grave. A grim little smile curved the corners of Dick's mouth as the simile occurred to him. Raising his hand, he knocked sharply with the little brass knocker and waited. There was no reply and, after a few moments, he knocked again. Still all was silent.

He pressed his shoulder against the door, but it was firmly shut and refused to give a fraction of an inch. He turned to Cowles, who stood at his side. 'We can't very well break the door down,' he said. 'It's too solid for one thing, and it would take too long for another. We had better try the window.'

They passed out from the vestibule and, stepping over the low wire fence that lined the side of the main pathway, found themselves upon a narrow strip of grass that ran beneath the window. Dick looked up and saw that the upper sash was open about an inch at the top. Placing his hands on the sill, he gave a quick spring and hoisted himself up. Pausing a moment, he glanced between the opening of the curtains, but could see nothing but blackness inside. Pushing his fingers against the upper bar of the lower sash, he pressed upwards. After one sharp protesting little squeak, the window opened easily enough, and Dick, moving aside a little table that stood in his way, dropped gently into the room. He turned and, leaning out of the open window, spoke to Cowles.

'If you go round to the front, I'll open the door for you,' he said. The inspector nodded and Dick, drawing back into the room, proceeded to try and make his way to the door.

The place was in pitch darkness, and twice he almost collided with a chair as he groped his way across in the direction he thought the door would be. Presently his outstretched hand, feeling along the wall, came in contact with the jamb of the door. He felt upwards along the wooden moulding in search of the electric light switch, which he guessed would be somewhere near. He found it and pressed it down. Instantly the room became flooded with light, softened as it streamed from beneath a large multicoloured silk shade that hung in the centre of the ceiling.

Dick took a swift look round and, as his eyes rested on the fireplace, he uttered a sharp exclamation of horror. Lying face downwards in the fender was the body of a man; his head and shoulders were covered with blood, which was still wet and glistened in the electric light. On the hearthrug at his side lay a heavy poker, bent and twisted and also bloodstained, with which obviously the man's head had been battered in.

Dick hurried along the passage and opened the door to admit Cowles. 'Come in quick,' he said tersely, and led the way back into the sitting room. 'You see that the Hooded Terror wasn't bluffing when he said he'd treated Wallace the same way as Blackie Phrynne,' he said to the inspector, pointing to the thing on the hearth.

Cowles's breath whistled through his

set teeth as he looked. 'Bludgeoned to death,' he said softly, and an extract from the records of Hammer Stevens that he had been reading that afternoon rose unbidden to his mind.

Dick, his face white, crossed over to the body and gently turned it over. The face was set in a rictus of agony and terror. Even Cowles, inured as he was to such sights, failed to suppress a shudder as he looked at it.

'It's Wallace right enough, and he's quite dead,' said Dick. 'The back of his head has been smashed to a pulp!'

Something white in one of the dead hands attracted his attention, and he bent closer. The fingers were closed round a white envelope. He gently disengaged it from the nerveless clasp, and found in doing so that the hands were still warm. The Hooded Terror must have rung up immediately after committing his horrible crime, and Dick wondered again at the slyness and audacity of the man.

The flap of the envelope had not been stuck down, and slipping his fingers into the opening he withdrew a slip of paste-board the size of a visiting card. He read the pencilled words on it and handed it to Cowles. Over the familiar sign of the Hooded Terror ran the message: 'Heed my warning or you will be next!'

Cowles looked grave as he read. 'I don't think you're going to have a very pleasant time,' he commented.

Dick shrugged his shoulders. 'I shan't lose any sleep over it,' he answered.

'At the same time, I should advise you to take precautions,' said Cowles. 'We have enough evidence — ' He nodded his head in the direction of the grim remains on the floor. ' — to show that the Hooded Terror doesn't make idle threats.' He looked round the comfortable sitting room. 'I wonder what Wallace did that necessitated his being killed?' he said musingly, and stared thoughtfully at the carpet.

Dick set about making a close examination of the room, but at the end of half an hour he had found nothing that was likely to provide a clue to the identity of the Hooded Terror. As usual, he had left not a scrap of evidence behind.

'I suppose we'd better notify Head-quarters,' he suggested at length. Cowles agreed, and went out into the little hall to the phone.

While Cowles was getting through to Scotland Yard, Dick continued his inspection of the flat. In the bedroom he found the hold-all of burglar's tools that Cowles had seen Wallace pocketing on the night of the burglary at Lathbury's. It had been thrust beneath a pile of handkerchiefs and collars in the wardrobe.

A small safe that stood in one corner was open, apparently having been opened with Wallace's own keys, for the bunch still dangled in the lock. But it was empty, not so much as a scrap of paper having been left in the interior.

Dick searched the place thoroughly, but he found nothing of interest, although there was plenty of evidence to have convicted Wallace several times over for burglary.

He returned to the sitting room, after taking a hasty look round the little kitchenette, and making sure that there was nothing he had overlooked. Against the wall opposite the window was a desk that was combined into a bookcase. Dick went over to it and let down the flap. The inside was stuffed full of letters and documents, and had apparently already been overhauled, for the papers were bundled in anyhow in an untidy heap. They were mostly bills, and several letters in a woman's writing that were signed 'Lydia', whom Dick knew was the dead crook's wife. But if there had been anything else there, it had already been taken by the man who had killed Wallace.

He had just completed an inspection of the last bundle, a heap of receipts, when Cowles returned from the phone. 'They're sending a man down from the Yard to take charge,' announced the inspector. 'We shall have to wait here until he arrives.' He looked at the open desk. 'Found anything?' he enquired.

Dick shook his head. 'Nothing,' he said. 'I was hoping that we might come across the envelope that was stolen from Lathbury's, but there's no sign of it.'

'I didn't expect you'd find that,' replied

Cowles. 'In my opinion that was the reason Wallace was killed.'

Dick looked up quickly. 'To obtain the envelope?' he asked. Cowles nodded his head slowly. 'But the Hooded Terror sent him to get it,' Dick protested. 'The usual card was left on Lathbury's desk.'

'Possibly,' agreed Cowles. 'But that doesn't say that Wallace handed the envelope over.'

'But why should he keep it?' said Dick in a puzzled voice. 'As Lathbury said, it was of no value.'

'It was of sufficient value,' replied the inspector, 'for the Hooded Terror to take the trouble of sending Wallace to break in to get it; and my idea is that Wallace discovered what that value was and held on to it.'

'But what possible value could there be in a list of securities?' argued Dick. 'It wasn't as if it had been the securities themselves. I could understand it then, but — '

'I think,' said Cowles, 'that in some way that envelope contained a clue to the identity of the Hooded Terror. Mind you, it is only a theory of mine, but I think Wallace found out what it was and was killed to keep the secret.' He paused and added, 'I'd like to know where Morrison was at the time that call was put through to you at the Yard.'

'I believe you suspect Morrison of being the Hooded Terror!' cried Dick.

'The list of securities,' answered Cowles, 'were Morrison's, and he was the only person who could have known whether or not they contained anything else besides just a plain, straightforward list.'

Dick was thoughtfully staring at the open desk, but his mind was so occupied that he wasn't even aware of its existence. Was it possible that the cheery, round-faced Morrison, with whom everybody joked and laughed, and voted the best of good fellows, the star reporter of the *Monitor*, could be the sinister criminal who concealed his identity so successfully under the soubriquet of the Hooded Terror, and whose many crimes had shocked the civilized world? It seemed incredible, and yet . . .

Suddenly Dick turned to Cowles. 'You've forgotten one thing,' he said. 'On the night Blackie Phrynne was killed, Morrison was with us in my flat.'

'Yes, I had forgotten that,' admitted Cowles. 'But at the same time, there's no proof that the Hooded Terror himself murdered Phrynne. It might have been one of his gang who actually did the deed.'

'I don't agree with you there,' said Dick, shaking his head. 'I am positive that he struck down Phrynne with his own hand.'

'Well, anyway, I am setting a man on to watch Mr. Jack Morrison,' said Cowles, 'and I've got an idea that he won't be wasting his time either!'

Shortly after, an inspector arrived from headquarters, bringing with him the divisional surgeon, whom he had picked up on his way. After Dick had briefly acquainted them with the facts that had led to the discovery of the murder, and complied with the formalities demanded by the law on such occasions, he and Cowles took their departure.

Dick had some reports to complete at the Yard before going home, and he took leave of Inspector Cowles at Piccadilly Circus. Passing down the Haymarket on his way to Whitehall, his thoughts still busy with Cowles's suspicions of Jack Morrison, he happened to look up suddenly.

On the opposite side of the street, a man and a girl were walking slowly along, deep in earnest conversation. As they passed beneath an electric light standard, Dick gave a gasp of surprise and stopped dead. For the man was Last Minute Morrison, and the girl he was talking to so earnestly was Christine Baker!

10

Lydia Speaks Her Mind

Lydia Stepping lay back on the soft lace-edged pillows of her bed in the exquisitely appointed bedroom in her luxurious flat in Victoria Street, and sipped daintily at the cup of tea that had just been brought her by her maid. The morning paper was as yet unopened, for Lydia was not a great news reader, and it lay on the silken coverlet by her hand.

For some time she lay still and gazed contentedly round the pretty room. Then, having finished her tea, she set the cup down; and reaching out her hand to the little table that stood beside the bed, she selected a cigarette from the silver box which lay there. Lighting it, she sank back once more among her pillows, blowing a cloud of blue smoke ceiling-ward from between her red lips.

Presently, from sheer boredom, she picked up the paper and began to glance lazily at its contents. Her scream a few seconds later brought Julia, her maid, hurrying in with a startled face. Her mistress was sitting bolt upright, still clutching the paper in shaking hands, her face white and bloodless, and her eyes wide and staring with fear and horror.

'What is the matter, madam?' cried the maid. 'Are you ill?'

'Get me some brandy — quick,' croaked her mistress in a husky voice. While the frightened maid hurried on her errand, Lydia looked again at the paragraph in the paper that had forced the scream from her throat.

The heading ran in big type:

ANOTHER HOODED TERROR CRIME.
TRAGEDY AT CAMBERLY MANSIONS.

With eyes that were blurred with unaccustomed tears, Lydia read the short account of the murder. Strange as it might seem, in spite of their unconventional mode of life she had been genuinely in love with her husband, and the sudden shock produced by the bald account of his death had for the moment paralyzed her faculties.

She was not an ordinary girl, however. Her life, lived for the most part among surroundings where incidents of this kind were an everyday occurrence, had taught her to stifle and check her natural emotions, so that by the time Julia returned with the brandy, she had managed at least outwardly to regain something of her former calmness.

She took the glass from the maid's hand and drank the contents at a single draught. The potent spirit acted almost immediately, and slowed the rapid beating of her heart, so that the hand that set the empty glass down was trembling less visibly.

'Is madam feeling better?' asked Julia anxiously as she hovered round the bed.

'Yes,' answered Lydia, striving to keep her composure. 'It was silly of me, wasn't it? Help me to dress, Julia. I must go out at once.'

The maid helped her into a silken wrap as she stepped out of bed. 'What made you scream?' she asked curiously.

Lydia had to think of some excuse quickly. It was impossible to tell the maid the truth, for Julia did not even know that she was married. At the flat she was known as Miss Benson.

'Just nerves, I think,' she answered with a forced laugh that sounded hollow, a weird travesty of mirth.

She could have screamed again as the maid flittered about the room and questioned her as to what she would like to wear. What did it matter what she wore? Nothing mattered. She dressed hurriedly in a sort of dazed dream, with a dull ache at her heart, and all her senses throbbed and echoed with the one idea that had taken possession of her brain, one fixed resolve.

She would get the man who had robbed her of all she had ever cared for. She would devote the rest of her waking existence to that sole purpose. It might take her months, it might take her years, but in the end she would get him!

She waved aside Julia's suggestion of breakfast. She felt that the very sight of food would choke her, and hurried out into the street.

A taxi was crawling past the door. Hailing it, she jumped inside after instructing the driver to drive to Scotland Yard.

Inspector Cowles was waiting for Dick when she was shown into his office by a wondering sergeant. 'Mrs. Wallace!' he said in surprise as he saw her, and signalled to the sergeant to leave them.

'Mrs. Stepping,' she corrected, and was astonished with herself for bothering about such a trivial matter as a name. 'Stepping was Harry's real name. May I sit down? You can guess why I've come, can't you?'

He nodded and dragged forward a chair. She sank into it gratefully, feeling that her trembling limbs would not have supported her a second longer.

'I saw the account in the paper,' Lydia Stepping said to Inspector Cowles. 'It was a terrible shock — stunning!' Her voice broke in the middle; she ended in a husky whisper.

Cowles saw the tears well up in her eyes in spite of her obvious efforts to keep calm. He felt surprised, for he had never believed that there was anything more between Stepping and his wife than a matter-of-fact business compact.

'You have my deepest sympathy,' he said, and meant it.

'Thank you,' she answered, 'but please don't talk like that or I shall break down.'

He saw that she was putting up a tremendous effort, and using all her willpower to stop herself from crying.

'Have you got any clue to the man who — who killed him?' she asked tonelessly.

'Beyond the fact that we know it was the Hooded Terror, no,' he answered her.

Her lips compressed into a hard line, and her eyes glistened as he mentioned the name. 'I don't know much,' she said, 'but what I do know may help you. Harry rang me up the other night and asked me to meet him at Victoria — '

'I know,' said Cowles. 'I followed you.'

'He told me,' she continued rapidly, without taking any notice of his interruption, 'that he had stumbled by accident on a good thing, and handled properly it would mean thousands, and that both our fortunes would be made. He was getting tired of the life we had to lead, and wanted to settle down abroad.' The tears were very near but she choked them back. 'He would not tell me everything, but I gathered that, quite by chance, he had discovered the real identity of the Hooded Terror.'

'What!' shouted Cowles excitedly.

'Yes,' she went on, speaking jerkily. 'He said that he was a man who had occupied the next cell to him at Dartmoor some years ago, and had escaped.' The inspector leaned forward, a sudden gleam in his eyes. 'Harry would not tell me his name or anything about him. He said the knowledge was too dangerous for me to share, but he had seen him recently in London. He said that he was going to make quite sure that night, and that the proof of his suspicions was at a Mr. Lathbury's house. He was going to burgle

136

it, and if he could lay his hands on this proof he was going to demand a large sum of money from the Hooded Terror to keep the secret of his identity. Harry said he was in the position to pay, and that the thing would be easy.'

'I see,' said Cowles softly, and he did. The reason for Sparkler Wallace's murder was clear, and his theory in that respect at least had been correct.

'He didn't give you any hint as to who the Hooded Terror was?' he asked.

She shook her head. 'Do you think I would be here if he had?' she demanded. 'If I knew that man, Inspector, at this moment I'd swing for him.'

Cowles heard the throb of hatred in her voice, and saw the sudden flash in her eyes and the set determination of her mouth, and he knew that the Hooded Terror had to reckon with a dangerous enemy in Lydia Stepping.

'I tried to make Harry tell me who it was,' she said presently, more calmly. 'But he wouldn't. I think he was afraid for my safety.' She leaned forward suddenly. 'Find the Hooded Terror before I do, if you want him to stand his trial,' she cried. 'For as sure as there's a God in heaven, I'll get him for what he did to Harry!'

The iron grip she had kept over her emotions for so long snapped, and she collapsed and broke into a fit of hysterical sobbing.

★　★　★

On the outskirts of Wimbledon, lying close to the south side of the common, is a broad avenue lined on either side by wide-spreading trees. The avenue is usually deserted, for it leads only to a narrow lane that runs across the end at right angles and is as little frequented as the avenue itself.

The houses on each side of the roadway are mostly empty, and are, to judge from the array of house agents' and auctioneers' boards that protrude shyly from the straggling hedges and trees, and that almost conceal them from the road itself, for sale. They are big houses, standing well back, and for the most part possessing crescent-shaped drives leading to their front entrances. For some reason or other they have missed the attentions of some enterprising builder who might otherwise have pulled them down and erected red-roofed monstrosities (under the facetious name of 'desirable modern residences, with every convenience') on this site, and remain great epitaphs of brick and stone, rising superior to suburbia, in memory of splendours long since dead.

The largest of these houses, a four-storey building of grey stone, and possessing more acreage than any of its fellows, was sited about halfway up the avenue on the right-hand side. From the roadway it was completely hidden, so heavily wooded were the grounds in which it stood. The only signs of habitation were the broken gates at the end of the weed-choked drive and the several 'for sale' boards that creaked dismally in the rising wind. The avenue was economically lighted, the lamp standards being few and far apart.

About ten o'clock on the night following the murder of Wallace, the quiet and shadowy street began to show signs of unusual activity. At intervals of some two or three minutes' duration, dim figures slunk along in the darkness — furtive shapes bred of the blackness of the night, evil and unclean. At a point coincident with the broken drive gates of the empty house, they seemed to melt away and vanish into the deeper shadows of the drive. Some were slouching and shabbily dressed, others upright and spruce, one or two evening-clothed and opera-hatted; but all were making for the same destination.

For in the old, dilapidated, empty house in that obscure avenue, the Hooded Terror held the first and last meeting of his servitors.

How he had obtained the keys — what careful manoeuvring must have been necessary to ensure that no two should arrive together — could only be guessed. But here again his organization was a triumph of attention to detail. Every member of his gang had received explicit instructions giving him the route he was to travel by, and the time he must arrive, so that the fact of so many arriving together was guarded against, and could not be remarked upon and give rise to suspicion.

As each one passed up the neglected drive and came to the dark entrance of the empty house, the door opened, admitted them, and closed again immediately they had entered the hall. A voice, sounding hollow and muffled, directed them to a room on the right, and a hand took their arm and guided them through the doorway. There was no light, and the velvety blackness was so dense that it could almost be felt.

When the last arrival had passed through the doorway and been piloted into the room on the right of the hall, there came the sound of a scraping match, and a feeble yellow glimmer pierced the intense darkness.

The man who held the match was dressed entirely in black, his head covered with a cowl-like mask of black silk. He lit an end of candle and, as the flame burnt up, gazed round the large, bare room at the mixed assembly before him. Truly the Hooded Terror had selected his agents from all branches and classes of life. The masked man set the end of candle on the mantelpiece and addressed the puppets who worked to the pull of the strings held in the hands of their unknown master and, from fear of the tragic consequences of disloyalty, remained loyal.

'I have called you all here tonight,' the Hooded Terror began in a high-pitched voice, 'to tell you that the time has come for us to disband. Things have happened that make it imperative for me to leave this country immediately, and before doing so I wish to thank all those who have been loyal to me.'

He paused and raised his voice slightly. 'I will not disguise the fact from you that we are in considerable danger. Facts that might have enabled the police to identify me have on two occasions almost come to light, but I took the necessary steps to safeguard myself, and the would-be traitors were punished.'

A little shudder passed through his listeners, for they knew that he was referring to Blackie Phrynne and Sparkler Wallace.

'I have upon my tracks,' continued the masked man, 'two of the cleverest officials at Scotland Yard who, I will admit, are a source of considerable anxiety to me. I am referring to Superintendent Richard Trent and Detective-Inspector Cowles. I am taking steps to remove Trent, for reasons not entirely connected with my personal safety, before I make my final getaway.' He paused again. 'There is, however, besides the two I have already mentioned, another man who shall be nameless, and who is to be more feared than either.'

He took from his pocket several white packets. 'I have here,' he went on, 'your share of the proceeds of our last two — er — operations.' He handed each of the men present one of the packets. 'I have added a substantial bonus. I may have to call upon some or all of you for assistance in the near future; if so, you will receive your instructions in the usual way. That is all. You will now leave singly, following the orders you have already received as to the method of your return. Go!'

He waited until the last man had

passed out and the house was empty once more; then he removed the cowl from about his head, slipped it into the pocket of his long coat, and passed through the front door, locking it behind him.

A distant clock was striking eleven when the dim figure of a man turned out of the drive gates and hurried away towards the end of the avenue, which led into a road that ran in the direction of the station. As he passed beneath a street lamp the light shining full on his face revealed his identity. It was Last Minute Morrison!

11

The Electric Light Globe

Jack Morrison was descending the steps of the offices of the *Daily Monitor* on the following morning when he saw Dick Trent approaching in the distance, and went to meet him.

'Hello,' said Dick as they shook hands. 'I was looking for you, Jack. Let's go somewhere where we can talk.'

Morrison led the way down a side street to a little café, and it being before the lunch-hour rush they found no difficulty in securing a table in a quiet corner.

'Now,' said Dick when they were seated and the waitress had brought the coffee he had ordered, 'I want to ask you one or two questions.'

Morrison regarded him for a moment steadily, in silence, while a quizzical smile played about the corners of his mouth. 'Fire away,' he said at length. Lighting a cigarette, he leaned back in his chair.

'Well, in the first place then,' began Dick, resting one elbow on the marble-topped table, 'was there anything in that list of securities that was stolen from Lathbury's that was likely in any way to give a hint to the identity of the Hooded Terror?'

'Not as far as I know,' he replied. 'Why? What makes you think there may have been?'

'I am asking the questions at the moment,' said Dick with a smile, and the reporter grinned. 'Did you make out the list yourself?' Morrison nodded. 'Where?' asked Dick.

The star reporter of the *Monitor* thought for a moment before replying. 'At the office, I think,' he answered. 'Yes, I remember. I made the rough list out at home and brought it down to the office to make a typed copy before giving it to Lathbury.'

'It wasn't even in your own handwriting, then?' said Dick. When Morrison shook his head, he felt that the information he had hoped to gain left a lot to be desired.

He sipped his coffee before putting his next question. 'Jack,' he said suddenly, 'of whom are you afraid?'

Morrison stared at him for a moment, and his eyes narrowed slightly. 'What exactly do you mean?' he demanded.

'You wear a bullet-proof waistcoat and carry two guns,' said Dick quietly. 'A man doesn't do that unless he's afraid of somebody.'

'You forget,' answered Morrison, laughing, 'that I have been commissioned by the *Monitor* to find the Hooded Terror, and I am not particularly anxious to stop any stray bullets that may be knocking around. He doesn't seem to care very much where they go.'

'Is that the only reason?' persisted Dick.

'Well, personally,' replied Morrison, with a twinkle in his eyes, 'I think it's a very excellent one. I don't wish to emulate the dead and be snatched from this world in the flower of my youth.'

Dick leant forward across the table. 'Listen here, Jack,' he said, 'be serious for a moment. You and I have known each other for some time. I'm also out to get the Hooded Terror, but I believe you know a lot more about him than I or any of us do.'

'If that's so, perhaps it's because I'm so interested,' said Morrison.

'But why are you so interested?' asked Dick in a puzzled voice.

'You'll know that,' said Last Minute Morrison, flickering the ash from his cigarette, 'when you learn the identity of the Hooded Terror.'

'Do you know it?' Dick shot the question suddenly.

'I think I do,' said the reporter softly. 'It's been a long chase, but it's nearly over. It's only a question now of whether I can get him before he gets me.'

'Do you mean he's trying to kill you?' asked Dick in amazement.

'He's been trying to kill me for the last twelve years!' said Morrison. 'And the only thing that's stopped him is the fact that he can't locate me.'

'Who is he?' demanded Dick.

'If I told you who I thought he was, you'd only laugh at me,' he replied. 'And the only proof I've got is a small piece of paper covered with a meaningless pencilled scrawl.' He eyed the table thoughtfully. 'Leave it at that, Dick. The time's coming, and coming soon, when you'll know everything.'

He threw away his cigarette, putting out the smouldering stump by setting his heel on it. 'I wish I had the Hooded Terror in the same position,' he said primly, and Dick was astounded at the sudden note of venomous hate that had sprung into his usually good-natured voice.

It was obvious that Morrison could have said a lot more if he had liked, and Dick felt irritated at his silence. Wherever he turned, he was met with a blank wall of secrecy. Even Christine. As the thought of the girl entered his mind, he remembered the fact of his having seen her with Morrison, walking down the Haymarket on his way to Scotland Yard after leaving Maida Vale.

'I saw you the other night with Miss Baker,' he said. 'Have you known her long?'

'You're more full of questions than a politician this morning,' said Morrison, raising his eyes from his cup. 'Yes, I've known Christine for a considerable time — ever since she was a baby, in fact. Why?'

'I only wondered,' said Dick shortly, and was annoyed with himself for the sudden little spasm of jealousy that shot through him.

There seemed to be nothing more to be got out of the reporter, so after a further and equally fruitless attempt to draw information from him, Dick gave it up and returned to the Yard.

He had not been in his office five minutes before he received a message from the assistant commissioner to see him at once. Dick had been expecting the summons. He walked into the assistant commissioner's office with a feeling very like that of a man going to the scaffold.

For over half an hour his grey-haired superior talked, and the things he said were not pleasant. 'It comes to this,' he concluded at length. 'In the space of a week, two men have been murdered — one literally on your own doorstep — and nothing has been done to apprehend the murderer, or any clue been furnished as to his identity. It's bad, Trent, very bad, and unless you can do something definite with regard to this Hooded Terror within the next week, I shall have to put the case in the charge of someone else. I hate having to say this, but there it is.'

Dick returned to his own office later in a frame of mind that was anything but pleasant. For the rest of the day he occupied himself with minor matters; routine work that, uninteresting as it was, had to be done. About the middle of the afternoon, he rang up the Western and Union Bank and arranged with Christine to take her out to dinner. He felt better after that, and the prospect of spending a cheerful evening with the girl did much to lift his despondency.

Of Cowles there was no sign all day. It was not until Dick was on the point of going home that that immaculate man put in an appearance.

'Where have you been all day?' said Dick as he came into the office.

Cowles crossed to the desk and helped himself to a cigarette. 'I've spent the day trying to find out where the man who was the governor of Princetown Convict Prison at that time is at the present time,' he replied.

'And where is he?' asked Dick as he pulled on his coat.

'Dead,' said Cowles, briefly and disgustedly. 'So I had my trouble for nothing.'

'And supposing he'd been alive,' said Dick, 'what did you expect to learn?'

'Just by what means he was able to identify the body that was found on that farm on the edge of Dartmoor as that of Hammer Stevens,' answered Cowles.

Dick laughed. 'Are you still trying to prove that Stevens is alive?'

The inspector nodded his head doggedly. 'More so than ever, since I've heard Lydia's story,' he replied. 'And I've certainly discovered something today that bears out my theory, anyhow.'

'What's that?' asked Dick interestedly.

'The man who occupied the next cell to Sparkler Wallace at Dartmoor — and whom, according to Lydia, he saw and recognized recently in London — was Hammer Stevens,' Cowles replied triumphantly.

Dick stared at him in amazement. 'There must be some mistake,' he said doubtfully. 'Who was in the cell on the other side?'

'There wasn't any other side,' said the inspector. 'Wallace's cell was the last, at the end of H Ward. There was only a blank wall on the other side.'

The news was startling, and Dick turned it over in his mind on his way home. If Stevens was still alive, whose had been the body that had been identified as his? There was only one answer to that question. It must have been Arkwright's, the man who was suspected of having killed him.

As Dick reached the door of his flat and was feeling for his key, a man came up the stairs behind him. Dick turned swiftly, mindful of the Hooded Terror's threat and wary of attack, but it was only Albert.

'Where have you been?' asked Dick as they stepped into the hall and switched on the light.

'Somebody rang up, sir,' said Albert wrathfully, 'and said that my sister had met with a serious accident. I hurried to her place at once, and found that it was all a stupid practical joke.'

Dick experienced a sudden sensation of danger. Albert had preceded him down the little hall while he had been speaking, and was in the act of opening the sitting room door when Dick's warning cry reached him. But it was too late! His hand was already on the light switch; and as he pressed it down, there came a deafening explosion that lifted him off his feet and flung him back into Dick's arms. A pungent smell of burnt cordite filled the hall, and a wave of acrid smoke caught Dick by the throat and nearly choked him.

Albert was a hanging dead weight in his arms, the blood pouring from a gaping wound in the front of his head. Dick laid him gently down on the floor and wiped his smarting eyes with his handkerchief. There was a sound of feet upon the stairway outside, and the door of the flat, which Dick had not time to close, was flung open. The plain-clothes man whom Cowles had set to trail Dick appeared, asking anxiously, 'What's happened, sir? I heard the noise in the road. It sounded like an explosion. What was it?'

'It was a bomb!' replied Dick grimly, and he told the man what had happened. 'I'm afraid my servant's badly hurt,' he added. 'You'd better get a doctor.'

The detective nodded and went out. The landing was full of startled tenants who had flocked to discover the meaning of the noise that had shaken the building. The Yard man explained briefly and sent them back to their various homes, with the assurance that everything was all right.

Albert's wound proved more serious than Dick had imagined, for the doctor on arriving discovered that a small portion of bone from the front of the skull had been driven into the head and was pressing on the brain. An ambulance was sent for, and Albert was conveyed to hospital. It was not until all these preliminaries had been attended to that Dick got a chance to examine the room in which the explosion had occurred. Not an article of furniture remained whole, not a pane of glass in the windows. Every pane had been cut clean out as if by a knife, and the carpet in the centre of the room was smouldering. This he extinguished with a jug of water, and then he stepped gingerly about the shattered room, looking for fragments.

The bomb had exploded immediately Albert had turned on the light. There must have been some connection, thought Dick, and presently he found it — a piece of metal with two projecting points. He looked at it for a moment, wondering what it reminded him of. Then in a flash the solution came to him. It was the facsimile of the butt of an electric light globe!

That was what had happened. During Albert's absence, someone had entered the flat and substituted a bomb for the light globe in the sitting room. The turning on of the current had fired the explosive it contained. It was an ingenious idea, and had he been the first to enter the room — which he usually was — it might easily have attained its object. But the Hooded Terror for once had failed!

Having finished his investigations and stuck a strip of plaster over a long cut on his face, he phoned up Cowles. 'Our friend has started,' he said, 'and he nearly got me.'

There was the sound of a soft whistle at the other end. 'You've got to be careful,' said Cowles, after Dick had explained. 'If I'm right and he is Hammer Stevens, you've got to remember that you're dealing with a wild beast! He's got half a dozen murders behind him and the grey doors of the death-house in front. And they can only hang him once! It's better to figure in the witness-box than on the indictment. Where are you going to stay tonight?'

'Here,' answered Dick. 'It's only the sitting room that has suffered.'

'Well, I'm going to send you a man from the Yard to take the place of Albert,' said Cowles, 'and two more to watch the place back and front.'

'I don't think he'll try again tonight,' said Dick. 'I shall be very surprised if he does.'

'You never know,' said the practical Cowles, 'and we won't take any risks. If it *is* Hammer Stevens, I shouldn't be surprised at anything!' And he rang off.

12

A Dinner for Two

In the midst of the excitement, Dick remembered his appointment with Christine and hurriedly dressed. His bedroom, which adjoined the sitting room, had suffered little damage from the explosion, save for a slight bulging of the wall.

He had arranged a pleasant little dinner for the evening, and he was looking forward eagerly to his meeting with the girl whose future absorbed the whole of his attention and thoughts. For the moment even the Hooded Terror had faded into the background, and might have been forgotten altogether were it not for the fact that Christine was so inextricably mixed up with the mystery that he couldn't think of one without thinking of the other.

He had promised to call for her at seven o'clock, and he finished tying his dress bow with one eye on the clock. It was five past seven before the taxi set him down at the entrance to the block of flats in which she lived. It was the first time Dick had been there. He wondered for a moment how the girl could possibly manage to keep up such an expensive establishment on the salary she received as James Lathbury's secretary.

Christine opened the door herself, and Dick, who had never seen her before in evening clothes, was smitten dumb by her beauty. She wore a simple dress of black charmeuse, innocent of colour except for a touch of gold at her waist. It set off the milky whiteness of her neck and shoulders, and threw into vivid relief the spun gold of her hair. She looked taller, to Dick's eyes, and the sweetness of her flower-like face was a benison which warmed and comforted his heart; and it seemed to Dick as if he had known this girl for a lifetime.

'Well,' she said with a smile as he looked at her, 'am I presentable?'

'You're wonderful,' breathed Dick, and the admiration in his voice sent a wave of colour mantling her cheeks. She experienced a thrill of triumph and happiness that she had impressed him so.

In the cab on the way up Piccadilly he sat stiffly in one corner, lest the substance of this beautiful dream should be touched by his irreverent hands. She was to him the spirit and embodiment of all that womanhood means. She was the living incarnation of the dreams that men dream, the divine substance of all the shadowy ideals that haunt their thoughts.

'How did you get that cut on your face?' asked the girl after they had been ushered by an obsequious headwaiter to a corner of the big dining room of the Carltonian.

Dick raised his hand and gently stroked the strip of pink court plaster. 'It was a little present from the Hooded Terror,' he replied lightly, and told her about the electric light bomb that had wrecked the sitting room of his flat. 'It sounds dreadfully melodramatic, doesn't it?' he said laughingly. 'I find great difficulty in reconciling the happening to the realities of life. Lately I seem to be living in the atmosphere of Lycaeum drama.'

Her face had gone white when he told her of the incident, and her large blue eyes were fixed on him with a scared expression in their depths. 'Oh, but it's terrible,' she murmured. 'Surely something can be done to put a stop to the outrages of this dreadful man. Haven't you any idea who he is?'

Dick shook his head. 'Not the faintest,' he confessed. 'I can't get hold of even the slightest resemblance to a clue. By the way,' he added inconsequentially, 'I didn't know that you knew Jack Morrison.'

She seemed embarrassed at his sudden question. Her eyes dropped to her plate, and her cheeks went pink. 'Yes. I know him,' she answered haltingly. 'He — he is a friend of mine. I've known him for some time. How did you know?'

'I saw you with him yesterday,' said Dick, feeling suddenly miserable.

'I forgot you were a detective,' she said laughing, but he could see that the subject was not a pleasant one to her, and was sensible enough not to pursue the conversation further. But he could not check the sharp twinges of jealousy that shot through him as he noticed her confusion at the mention of Morrison's name.

'Has Lathbury been annoying you again?' he asked, to change the subject.

She smiled. 'No,' she replied. 'He's back again at the bank, of course, but he hasn't said anything more. He looks too ill, poor man, to think of anything but doctors. However, I've told him I'm leaving at the end of the month.'

'What did he say?' said Dick.

'He seemed very concerned,' she answered, 'and begged me to reconsider my decision. But when he discovered that I wouldn't change my mind, he was awfully nice about it, and said he hoped I had a comfortable post to go to.' Dick smiled as she mimicked the pompous tones of the stout banker. 'As a matter of fact, I shan't be working again,' she continued. 'I'm going away for a long holiday. I told him so.'

Dick looked at her blankly. 'You — you're going away?' he stammered. She nodded. 'When are you going?' he asked, his castle of dreams suddenly tumbling about his ears.

'In a fortnight,' she answered, and was secretly delighted at the look of consternation which she surprised in his eyes.

'I shall miss you horribly,' he said simply.

She did not make the conventional remark that he had not known her long enough. As a matter of fact, it never entered her head, for although their acquaintance had been a comparatively short one, Dick already held a place in her life that she knew would be difficult to fill.

A little silence fell between them. Almost subconsciously, Dick stretched out his hand, and it rested for a moment over hers. She did not attempt to withdraw her own until a waiter came in sight, and then she drew it away so slowly as to suggest reluctance.

'Christine,' he said gently, when the waiter had again passed out of hearing, 'when you come back I have something I want to tell you. May I?' His hand again sought hers under cover of the table.

The colour came and went in her face; the soft, rounded bosom rose and fell more quickly than was usual; and the hand that he held lightly closed so tightly upon his fingers that they were almost numb when she suddenly released her hold. But she kept her eyes averted and he couldn't see the expression on her face. She did not speak for such a long time that he began to be afraid be had offended her.

'I'm going away for a very long time,' she murmured at last, in so low a voice that Dick had to lean towards her to catch the words. 'Must you wait until I come back be-before you tell me?'

She turned her face to his, and he saw that her eyes were bright with unshed tears. Something in Dick's throat made it impossible for him to speak for the moment.

'If you're not very careful,' she said, with an attempt at raillery, 'I shall propose to you.'

Dick never remembered quite what he said then, but he poured out all that had been pent up in his heart, and more, while Christine listened with shining eyes and glowing cheeks. If he had asked her at that moment to run away with him, to commit the maddest folly, she would have consented joyously; for her love for the man was surging up within her like the bubbling stream of subterranean fire that had found its vent, overwhelming and burning all reason, all tradition.

The time seemed to speed by on winged feet, and it was with a start of surprise that Dick presently discovered it was ten o'clock.

During the journey back to Christine's flat in the taxi, they were both strangely silent; Dick dreaming of the golden future that awaited him, and the girl intoxicated with the happiness that had so suddenly come into her life.

At the entrance to the block he dismissed the taxi, electing to walk back home.

For a long time they stood outside the flats, talking about nothing in particular but finding it of vast importance to themselves. At last Christine held out her hand.

'I must go now, Dick,' she said softly. 'I shall shock the neighborhood if I stay talking to you any longer.'

It was the first time she had called him by his Christian name, and Dick felt absurdly proud of the fact. He held her little gloved hand in his for a long time, reluctant to let her go. Then, glancing up and down the street to make sure that it was deserted, he drew her towards him and bending down, kissed her . . .

'Good night, Christine,' he said in a low voice as she disengaged herself from his embrace.

'Good night, Dick,' she said, and waving her hand disappeared into the dimly lit entrance.

A man who had been watching from the shadow of a doorway on the opposite side of the road compressed his lips and looked after the tall form of Dick as he swung away down the street, with an evil glitter in his eyes.

Dick, on his way homeward, was so enveloped in the rosy clouds which had descended upon him that he was unconscious of time or space or direction, and it was purely mechanically that he followed the right route to his flat. It seemed to him that a miracle had happened that evening, and he felt that at any moment it was possible he might wake up and discover that the whole thing was unreal. He felt wonderfully happy and light-hearted, and whistled cheerily below his breath as he strode on.

If he had been able to see into the future, and learn all that was to happen before he saw Christine again, he would have rushed back to the girl's flat then and there to save her from the terrible menace that was at that moment preparing to creep up on her out of the blackness of the night!

13

The Terror by Night

Christine returned to her flat after leaving Dick, and it seemed to her as if she were walking on air. As she prepared her frugal supper and made herself a cup of tea, her thoughts were happy ones.

A new and splendid outlook had come into her life that seemed to banish all the fears and doubts she had felt, and the future held delightful vistas. Only one faint shadow overcast the golden hue of her dreams, and she resolutely put even that aside tonight, refusing to think of it.

The quietness of the flat appealed to her, although there had been times when it had got on her nerves and forced her out into the lighted streets to seek company in the jostling crowds that thronged the pavements. But tonight she was glad to be alone, for her thoughts were all the company she needed.

169

Having eaten her supper and cleared the things away, she sat down to write to Dick, though she told herself reprovingly that it was but a short time since she had seen him. All the same, she wrote, for love takes no heed of time, and logic is unknown to the lover.

There was a pillar-box at the corner of the street in which her flat was situated; and slipping on her hat and coat, she went out to post her letter. She wondered as she passed along the dark street what Dick was doing at the moment, and hoped he was thinking of her.

Having dropped the letter into the box, she returned to the flat, let herself in, locked and bolted the door, and sat down in her little sitting room with a work basket beside her to fill in the hour which separated her from bedtime by mending some stockings. So occupied, her mind was filled to the exclusion of all else by Dick Trent. It seemed almost too wonderful to be true that he should have singled her out from among all other women, and she felt a sudden thrill of elation at the thought.

The little clock on the mantelpiece striking twelve brought her back to earth, and with a happy sigh she laid aside her work and prepared to go to bed. She undressed slowly, and as she did so, for no reason at all, the thought of James Lathbury strayed across her mind. A little smile curved the corners of her mouth as she compared his laborious and obviously carefully rehearsed proposal to Dick's sudden and tempestuous love-making, the impetuosity of which had almost carried her off her feet.

She got into bed, and for a time tried to read, but the book seemed peculiarly dull and not nearly as interesting as her own thoughts, although on the previous night it had appeared quite a good story. Eventually she gave it up and, switching off the light, lay in the half-darkness — for the lights from a neighboring electric sign filled the room with a dim radiance — and let her mind roam at random over the events of the day. She was dozing when a distant clock struck one, and fell almost immediately afterwards into a sound sleep.

Suddenly she opened her eyes. Some slight noise had awakened her. She had been lying facing the wall, and now she turned quickly in the bed, her heart thumping madly in her breast. Her eyes went to the door leading to the little passage outside. She had shut it before going to bed, but had omitted to lock it. Now it was ajar, and slowly opening.

For a moment she lay still, paralyzed with terror. Then she suddenly sat up. 'Who's there?' she called, but the dryness of her throat rendered the sound a mere husky whisper.

There came into the shadowy doorway a figure, the sight of which choked back the scream she tried to utter before it could be released. It looked tall by reason of the tight-fitting black coat it wore, which reached almost to the heels, and the face and head were hidden beneath a hideous cowl-like mask of black silk.

'Who's there?' she managed to gasp again.

'Don't scream; don't move!' said the figure, and the voice was high and squeaky and sounded hollow and far away.

'What do you want?' she asked in a terrified whisper.

'I want you,' answered the masked man. He waited as though expecting her to speak, but she was incapable of answering him. 'I have wanted you for a long time,' he continued. 'Many men love you, Christine Baker: Trent, Lathbury, and myself — and I love you most of all!'

'Who are you?' she managed to whisper hoarsely.

'I am the Hooded Terror!' answered the intruder.

She felt a shiver of stark fear run down her spine. If only Dick were somewhere near! If only she could communicate with him!

The unknown man seemed to read her thoughts, for he laughed harshly. 'Trent cannot help you,' he said. 'No one can help you. I have watched you for weeks — months, and I have waited patiently. Once in every man's life comes the one woman whom he knows — feels — is destined for him, and for him only. You are that woman to me, and I mean to have you!'

173

He paused. She felt half-faint with sheer terror, and could only stare at him hypnotized, unable to move or speak.

'I want you,' he repeated, and advanced nearer towards the bed. 'Will you come with me willingly, or — '

'Oh, go away, please, go away,' she whispered imploringly.

'When I go, you go with me,' he answered.

'You're mad,' she gasped. 'You must be mad!'

'Will you come with me willingly?' he asked again.

'How can I?' She was trying desperately to recover her calmness. She must think clearly. She must! She must! 'What you ask is impossible. I don't know you.'

'No, you don't know me.' His voice was softer, scarcely audible. 'But you *shall* know me. You shall know me as your husband.'

'No! No!' she breathed, but he took no notice of her interruption and continued.

'I will give you everything in life you can desire — riches, jewellery. I will load you with diamonds and dress you in

174

beautiful clothes. You shall never know what it is to want for a single thing. Every wish of yours I will grant you, Christine, if you will only come with me.'

He stopped, and the black gloved hand that rested on the rail at the foot of the bed trembled visibly with the force of his pent-up emotion.

'Never! Never!' she cried in a half strangled voice. Her heart was pounding in her throat from fear, and she felt her momentary courage fast oozing away. She was nearly on the verge of tears.

'Very well,' he answered, and his voice was now harsh and grating. 'I have given you a chance. You can never say I did not. As you refuse to come willingly, you shall come because you must!' His hand went quickly to a pocket in the long black coat he wore, and when he withdrew it she saw it held something that glittered in the dim light from the electric sign outside. 'Get up,' he commanded. 'Get up and dress, and clothe yourself warmly, for the night is cold, and we are going on a long journey.'

She hesitated. The unknown intruder

repeated his command. She felt almost incapable of movement, but somehow she managed to reach for her dressing gown and drag it round her shoulders. Forcing her trembling limbs to obey the command of her brain, and fighting desperately to overcome the feeling of faintness which for a moment made the room spin round her as she moved, Christine rose.

'You need not be afraid,' said the masked man as she commenced hurriedly to dress herself. 'I shall not hurt you, provided you do as you are told.'

His voice seemed to come from a great distance away. She told herself that the whole thing was a nightmare, a figment of her imagination, a dreadful dream; that in the morning she would wake and find that it had been all unreal. Her terror was having the effect of dulling her faculties. Her brain felt numb. She moved mechanically as though under the influence of a drug. The horrible figure with its hideous cowled head seemed to grow larger, then smaller, then larger again.

Somehow or other she managed to scramble into her clothes, and at last was fully dressed. She felt a hand grasp her arm firmly and lead her towards the bed. She became conscious suddenly of a pungent, sickly odour that filled the room. For a second her brain cleared and she tried to scream, but even as she opened her mouth the chloroform pad was pressed tightly over her face.

She struggled feebly, but she was held in a grip of steel. A dense, velvety blackness descended upon her. Her senses fled, and mercifully she lost consciousness.

14

'Where is Christine?'

Richard Trent read Christine's letter, which had arrived by the morning's post, as he sipped the early cup of tea provided by the constable who was doing duty as his temporary valet. The man was moving noisily about in the kitchen, and Dick made a grimace as he heard a sudden crash of breaking glass, and cursed the fate that had caused him to lose such a perfect servant as the soft-footed and noiseless Albert.

The wind had risen during the night, and with it had come the rain, which was now pattering on the window panes and turning the gutters of the streets outside into miniature cataracts.

Dick read the girl's letter for the third time quite needlessly — for he already knew it almost by heart, folded it up as though it were some rare and precious manuscript — as indeed it was to him, and, springing out of bed, made his way to the bathroom.

He was splashing about in his bath when there came a vigorous and prolonged ringing at the front door bell. It was followed by the sound of voices raised in high altercation, and then by the sound of hurried footsteps coming along the passage. Then someone banged loudly and repeatedly on the bathroom door.

'Trent! I say, Trent! For God's sake, come out,' cried a voice. Although it sounded strained and unnatural, Dick recognized it with surprise as that of Jack Morrison.

'What's the matter?' he demanded. 'What do you want?'

'The Hooded Terror has got Christine,' shouted Morrison. 'Hurry up, man! Can't you understand how urgent it is?'

Dick's heart went suddenly cold and the blood receded from his face, leaving it white to the lips. For a moment he felt strangely dizzy, but by a supreme effort he managed to regain his composure. 'I'll be out directly,' he said, and his voice, to his astonishment, sounded quite calm. 'In the meanwhile, go and ring up Cowles. You'll find the number of his flat on the pad by the telephone if he isn't at the Yard. Tell him what's happened, and ask him to come here at once.'

He dried himself quickly and hurriedly dressed, and in less than five minutes he was in the kitchen, which had been turned temporarily into a living room.

The constable was clattering about in the scullery beyond. Morrison was pacing up and down, his hands clasped behind him, his face drawn and haggard. He stopped as Dick entered and swung round. 'Trent, this is terrible!' he cried. 'What can we do? Something's got to be done quickly. I feel almost crazy.'

'For heaven's sake, calm yourself,' said Dick. 'If we're going to do anything at all, we've got to keep our brains as clear as possible. If we once let our nerves get the better of us, we might as well throw up the sponge. It's only by clear thinking that we've got the ghost of a chance of finding her.'

Morrison dropped onto a wooden

chair, and Dick, crossing quickly to the dresser, poured out a stiff whisky and soda and carried it over to him. 'Drink this,' he said, sharply, 'and then tell me all about it.'

Morrison took the glass with a trembling hand and drained the contents at a gulp. Dick noticed for the first time that his clothes were torn and spattered with mud, and that one side of his hair was caked with what appeared to be dried blood.

'I might have saved her,' began Morrison, 'only I got a bang over the head that laid me out. I had been following the Hooded Terror all the evening.'

'Following him!' repeated Dick incredulously.

Morrison nodded impatiently and seemed annoyed at the interruption. 'Yes,' he replied. 'I told you I'd get him before you did. I followed him last night to Christine's flat. He spotted me in the yard at the back and hit me over the head. The blow he gave me must have been a pretty heavy one, for I was unconscious for some hours. When I recovered, I went straight to the girl's flat. Although I knocked and rang, there was no answer. Of course, he had got her away whilst I was unconscious. If I had not been such a confounded fool, I might have known he would attempt something like that.'

'You didn't actually go into the flat, then?' demanded Dick.

'No,' said Morrison. 'What was the use? If there had been any living souls inside, they would have come to the door. The noise I made was enough to wake the dead.'

Dick suppressed a shudder. 'You don't think it's possible — ' he began, his voice trembling slightly.

'Oh, you needn't be afraid of that,' broke in Morrison, reading his thoughts. 'He wouldn't kill her. That's not his game. But unless we can find her soon . . . There are things far worse than death.'

Dick guessed what he meant, and knew that if he was to remain cool, he daren't think of the possibility. And coolness was essential if Christine was to be saved.

'Did you get through to Cowles?' he asked suddenly.

'Yes,' replied Morrison. 'He's coming round at once.'

'As soon as he arrives,' said Dick, 'we'll go straight round to Christine's flat. Whatever investigations we make, we've got to begin there.'

'I wish to heaven he'd hurry up, then,' said Morrison, starting to his feet and pacing up and down the room again. 'Every minute wasted may mean the difference between success and failure.'

'Jack,' said Dick curiously, 'why won't you tell me the reason you've been trying so persistently to run the Hooded Terror to earth?'

Morrison paused in his walking and shot him a quick glance. 'I have no time to tell you now,' he said. 'It's too long a story — but I'll tell you one day. It'll be soon now, I think. But, first of all, we've got to find that girl.'

'You've got to tell me one thing, Jack,' said Dick. 'There is some mystery between you and Christine. I've known that for a long time. What is it?'

Morrison hesitated before replying. 'I suppose you might as well know,' he said at length. 'She's my niece.'

If he had intended to surprise Richard Trent, he succeeded admirably. 'Your niece?' he echoed incredulously.

'Yes. She's the daughter of my brother,' replied Morrison. 'I'll tell you the whole story some other time. In the meanwhile — '

There came a ring at the bell. 'Here's Cowles now,' said Morrison with relief. They hurried along the passage and opened the door to the immaculate inspector.

'I came straight away in a taxi,' he said without preliminary. 'And I've kept it waiting. We'd better go straight along to Miss Baker's flat now.'

A few seconds later they were in the taxi and racing down Piccadilly. As they drew up outside the block of flats where Christine lived, Dick sprang out almost before the cab had stopped. In the entrance hall he found a porter engaged in cleaning some brasses. He strode up to the man.

'Have you got a pass-key to all the flats in this building?' he asked.

The man looked surprised, but nodded his head.

'Give it to me,' said Dick.

'But,' the porter demurred, 'I'd lose my job.'

'Well, then, come up and open the door of Miss Baker's flat,' said Dick, and before the man had time to refuse, he added, 'I'm a police officer.'

Dick had to satisfy him concerning his authority before he could be persuaded to fetch his pass-key from his little office under the stairs and lead the way to the top floor.

'This is Miss Baker's flat,' he said as he inserted the key in the lock of the door on the right.

'Who occupies the other flat?' asked Cowles, pointing to another and similar door opposite.

'It's empty,' said the porter. 'The people moved out about a month ago.'

He turned the key and opened the door, and they entered the narrow passage. Cowles paused and sniffed the

185

air for a moment. 'Chloroform,' he said tersely.

The sitting room door was open, and they looked in. Everything was neat and tidy, and Dick passed on down the passage till he came to another door on the left. It was closed, and Dick paused for a moment wondering what was about to greet his eyes in the room beyond. Then he threw the door open. It was obviously Christine's bedroom, and the bed had evidently been slept in, for the clothes had been hurriedly flung aside. There was no sign of disorder, but the room seemed to convey in some indescribable manner a suggestion of violence. Here, too, the odour of chloroform was more pronounced.

As they advanced further into the room, Inspector Cowles gave vent to a little exclamation and, stooping, picked up a small object from the floor. As he straightened up and held it in his fingers, Dick glanced at it. It was a small bottle; the label 'Chloroform' was clearly visible.

'There's no doubt she was drugged,'

commented Cowles, slipping the bottle into his pocket. He glanced swiftly round the room. 'He evidently forced her to dress,' he continued. 'There are no signs of any clothes about. The question is, how did he get her away?'

Dick and Inspector Cowles left the bedroom and went on through a door at the end of the passage, then found themselves in a tiny kitchen. The window was wide open. Cowles stepped across to it and peered out. He withdrew his head a moment later and turned to Dick.

'That's the way he got in,' he remarked, 'and it's probably also the way he went out. There's an iron fire escape outside the window that leads down to a yard at the back, and there is a sooty footmark on the wall, which the rain has partly washed away.'

Dick turned to the porter, who had been hanging about the passage eyeing them curiously. 'Is there any way out of that yard?' he asked.

'Yes, sir,' said the porter. 'There's a small door that leads out into a side street. It's used during the daytime by the tradespeople. They come in that way to the service lift.'

'It is also kept locked at night, I suppose?' said Cowles.

'Yes, sir,' answered the man. 'I always lock it myself, just before I leave.'

'What time do you leave?' inquired Dick.

'Usually about eleven,' answered the man. 'Sometimes a little later.'

'So you would be ignorant of anything that happened after that hour?' asked Cowles.

The man nodded.

'Did Miss Baker stay in after she came home last night?' questioned Dick.

The hall porter scratched his head and thought for a moment. 'She went out to post a letter about eleven,' he replied. 'It might have been a bit earlier; I couldn't be quite sure. Anyway, I know it was about the time I was getting ready to lock up, because she came back just before I shut the main door.'

'You always lock the main door?' asked Cowles.

'Yes, sir,' answered the man. 'I lock the

main door at eleven, and if any of the tenants want to go out or come in after that, they use their pass-keys.'

'What about the back door?' asked Dick. 'Have they got pass-keys to that as well?'

'No,' answered the porter. 'Nobody ever uses it except the tradespeople.'

'Was it locked or unlocked when you arrived this morning?' questioned Dick.

The man screwed up his face in an effort to remember, then he slowly shook his head. 'To tell you the truth, I couldn't say, sir,' he replied candidly. 'It was shut, but whether it was locked or not, I don't know.'

There was nothing more to be learnt from the porter, and they turned their attention to subjecting every room to a careful scrutiny; but beyond the chloroform bottle, they found not the vestige of a clue that was likely to show where the girl had been taken to.

It was with a feeling almost amounting to despair that Dick finally left the flat and, accompanied by Cowles and Morrison, made his way to Scotland Yard.

There was nothing for him to do except make the usual notification to headquarters, and circulate a description of the girl to all stations.

Having set in motion all the complicated machinery of the law, which begins to work when anyone mysteriously disappears, Dick, who was feeling sick and ill with worry, sank wearily into his chair behind his big desk. Resting his chin on his hand, he tried to think the matter out calmly.

He had need of all his courage and resolution. Exerting all his will, he tried with a tremendous effort to sweep away all sentiment from his mind. He must persuade himself that he was merely a detective officer engaged in tracing the disappearance of a girl named Christine Baker. He felt that if he thought of her in any other way, he would go mad.

Cowles, who was watching him, felt a wave of sympathy for his chief, for Dick's face reflected the agony of his mind. Presently Dick raised his head and looked across at Last Minute Morrison.

'You said you knew the Hooded

Terror,' he said. 'Who is he?'

'He is a man,' answered Morrison, 'without pity, and without any kind of human feeling — a brute beast, with the brains of a genius.'

'But who is he?' persisted Dick.

'He is known, or rather *was* known, as Hammer Stevens,' replied Morrison.

Cowles leapt to his feet. 'I knew it!' he cried. 'I always said he was the Hooded Terror.'

'But Stevens is dead,' said Dick. 'He was murdered by Arkwright.'

Morrison shook his head. 'No, that's where all of you are wrong,' he answered. 'Gordon Arkwright was killed by Hammer Stevens. And for that reason I have sworn to get him.'

'Why?' asked Dick, as a sudden light broke in his mind.

'Because,' said Last Minute Morrison quietly, 'Gordon Arkwright was my brother!'

'Then,' cried Dick. 'Christine is — '

'Gordon's daughter,' replied Morrison.

'I'm beginning to see quite a lot of things,' said Dick softly, and at that moment the telephone bell rang sharply.

The others saw his face change suddenly as he listened. Over the wire came a woman's voice — Christine's voice — agitated and imploring. 'Dick,' it cried, 'Dick! Save me! I'm at — '

There came a sharp cry, followed by a sudden rasping sound, and — silence.

Dick Trent hung the receiver back on the hook and started to his feet, his face white.

'That call was from Christine,' he cried, 'and somebody has cut the wire!'

15

At One-Tree Farm

Christine Baker recovered her senses to the accompaniment of throbbing temples and an intolerable thirst. Her mouth was dry and her head ached violently. She felt ill and sick. At first she was too dazed to take much notice of her surroundings, but in a little while a wind blowing on her from somewhere made her head clearer, and she started to look about her.

She discovered to her surprise that she was in a large closed car, and from the swaying of the vehicle concluded that it must be travelling at a high speed. With a rush the events of the night crowded back through her mind, and she remembered the horrible visitor whom she had awakened to find in her room. The horror of the night, then, had been real. Through the glass ahead she could see dimly the figure that crouched over the wheel, and recognized the cowl-like covering that it wore over its head.

She must have been unconscious for a considerable time, for already the faint grey light that precedes the dawn vaguely illuminated the roadway ahead. She tried to raise a hand to her hot head and found that it was impossible, as her wrists had been bound securely behind her back. She moved her legs to see if they had been treated in the same way, but discovered that they were free.

Through the window in front she could see that they were running along a narrow country road lined on each side by high straggling hedges. In some places they stretched almost across the roadway, and she could hear the branches swishing against the sides of the car as it forced its way between. Where were they going? Where was the unknown man in front taking her?

She felt cold, and shivered violently as a gust of wind blew in on her from one of the open windows in front. She would have given almost anything at that moment for a cup of hot, strong tea.

On and on sped the car, the figure at the wheel motionless. The countryside through which they were passing seemed to grow wilder and more desolate. Presently it began to rain, and the glass of the windows became opaque with the drops. Christine could see nothing, but their speed never slackened.

Suddenly the car swerved sharply to the left, and she was almost thrown off the seat at the unexpected jolt. She managed to retain her balance, although the violence of the impact of her body with the side of the car bruised her shoulder. They were bumping over a rough and narrow cart track into which the car had turned through a break in the thick hedge, and presently it slowed down and stopped. The man in the driving seat got down and opened the door, signing for her to get out.

He caught her arm as she descended and led her through a broken five-barred gate into a ploughed field. The rain was lashing down in torrents and stung her face as it was driven by the wind across the waste ground, but it was refreshing, and she felt grateful for the cooling drops against her hot cheeks.

The man was still holding her arm tightly, and without a word he walked her quickly across the field. She stumbled, and would have fallen but for his supporting hand.

'Where are you taking me?' she asked at last. But the only reply was a chuckle from the figure at her side.

She wondered if she could wrench her arm free and make a dash for the car, but remembered that her hands were tied and it would be useless, even if she could outdistance her captor, which was unlikely. They tramped on doggedly, and she began to speculate what her fate was to be. Did this terrible man intend to kill her?

Her thoughts turned to Dick. Would he be able to arrive in time to save her? She had such implicit faith in him that she never for one moment believed that he would fail to find her. It couldn't be long before he discovered that she had disappeared.

In a little straggling plantation they

presently stopped by a wooden gate from which a narrow path twisted away among a thickly growing clump of trees. 'Wait,' said the Hooded Terror, and releasing her arm, he fumbled in the pocket of his coat. He then stooped down and unlocked the gate. Holding it open, he signed for her to pass through, and after she had done so he shut and relocked the gate. He took her arm again and led her up the little path, and presently they rounded a patch of bushes and came in sight of a tumbledown and straggling cottage. Underneath the low porch he again found a key and unlocked the front door. There was a click, and the hall became flooded with light. Christine felt vaguely astonished that such a place should be fitted with electric light.

The masked man's figure stood silhouetted in the doorway, and he beckoned her forward. She drew back hesitatingly, but he grasped her by the arm and dragged her into the interior, slamming and bolting the door behind her.

She looked about her, curiosity overcoming her fear. The hall was comfortably furnished. Everything was neat and tidy and scrupulously clean. Suddenly her eyes lighted on the last thing she had expected to see. On a table behind the door stood a telephone.

'Welcome to One-Tree Cottage — your new home,' said the hooded man as he turned from barring the door. He opened a door on the right of the hall and ushered her into a room furnished as a sitting room. The carpet was thick, and the pictures on the wall, though few, were good. The place looked unexpectedly luxurious and comfortable.

'Sit down,' he said, indicating an easy chair. 'You are probably hungry after your journey. I will prepare some breakfast.'

Almost mechanically she obeyed him. She had expected him to take off the cowl from his head, but in this she was disappointed.

For a moment he stood and surveyed her. 'You are very beautiful, Christine Baker,' he murmured, almost to himself. 'So beautiful that I am taking a great risk for your sake, and giving up much. But you are worth it.'

He advanced towards her and she shrank back in terror, but he only severed the cords that bound her wrists with a penknife that he took from his pocket. 'I will go and get some food,' he said, and the remark was so ordinary, so utterly banal, that she almost laughed. 'It is impossible for you to escape. We are miles away from anywhere.'

He opened the door and, passing through, closed it behind him. She heard the key turn in the lock. She rubbed her wrists, which the tight cords had numbed, and, listening, heard the sound of his footsteps receding in the distance as he went down the passage to somewhere at the rear of the cottage. She remembered the telephone in the hall and wondered if it was in working order. If she could only get at the instrument and send a message to Dick!

She looked to see if there was any way out of the room. She could see that the windows behind the curtains were heavily shuttered. Her eyes travelled slowly round the room, and then she noticed that there was another door, which evidently communicated with some other apartment.

She rose cautiously to her feet and tried the handle. It was locked, but, looking down, her heart gave a leap as she saw that the key was on the inside. She turned it gently, but the door still remained firm against her pressure. It had either been screwed up or was bolted on the other side.

With a little sigh of disappointment, she returned to her chair. She could hear the rattle of crockery from somewhere in the distance. The sound reminded her of the first meal she had had with Dick in the little restaurant in the city. She began to conjecture what he would be doing at that moment, and smiled as she realized that in all probability he was in bed and asleep. If only she could get to the telephone! She sat and racked her brains to try and think of some way by which she could elude her captor long enough to get the call through.

Suddenly an idea flashed across her mind. Would the key in the other door fit both? There was a faint chance that it might.

She went over to the door again and took the key from the lock. At the same instant she heard the sound of returning footsteps, and running back to her chair, she slipped the key down the bosom of her dress.

There was a click as a key turned in the lock and the masked man entered. He carried a cup of tea and a plate of sandwiches which he handed to her. She drank the steaming fluid gratefully, and felt better, but she didn't touch the food, for she felt it would choke her. He watched her until she had drained the cup.

'Well,' he said as he took it from her, 'have you decided?'

She looked questioningly at him. 'Have I decided what?' she whispered in reply.

'Whether you will come away with me willingly or remain here a prisoner,' he said, and she could see his hard eyes regarding her steadfastly through the slits in the silken head covering. 'I am being fair with you. I am offering you marriage.

You hate me now, but that feeling will change.'

'It will never change,' she replied steadily. 'I would rather die than go with you.'

'You love somebody else.' The voice was hateful, harsh and menacing.

'You have no right to ask me that,' she breathed.

'I am not asking,' said the hooded man. 'I'm making a statement. You love somebody else, and that somebody is Richard Trent.' He leaned forward. 'You are mine, you understand? Mine! I have never yet been thwarted in a desire, and sooner than Trent should have you, I will kill you! Do you understand?' The squeaky, high-pitched voice had risen still higher, almost to a shrill scream. But the next moment he had recovered his calmness. 'I will leave you to think it over,' he said. 'In half an hour I shall return. This is your final chance. I advise you for your own sake to come with me. The alternative . . . ' He paused. ' . . . will not be pleasant.'

He turned and left the room, locking

the door behind him. Christine waited until his footsteps had died away; then, listening intently, she stole across to the door. With a hand that trembled with excitement, she tried the key in the lock. There came a little grating noise, and it turned!

Murmuring under her breath a prayer of thankfulness, she opened the door softly. The whole place was silent; she couldn't hear a sound. On tiptoe she stole out into the passage. The light in the hall was still on. Cautiously she crept over to the telephone, and paused. Still silence!

Should she call Dick at his flat, or at Scotland Yard? She remembered he had said he was going to the Yard early that morning. In any case she could leave a message there, as there might not be anyone at the flat.

She lifted the receiver. It was some time before she got an answer from the Exchange, and she was in a fever of dread lest the masked man should return before she could get through. But presently a girl's voice enquired, 'Number please.'

As loudly as she dared, and praying

that he would not hear her, Christine replied: 'Scotland Yard, urgent.'

It seemed an eternity before a gruff voice answered, 'Hello.'

'Is Mr. Trent there?' she asked eagerly. 'I want to speak to Mr. Trent — it is urgent, very urgent! Please hurry . . . '

Again she waited while the minutes dragged by, and then with a gasp of relief she recognized Dick's voice. 'Who's that?' he asked.

'Dick!' she cried, forgetting all caution. 'Dick! Save me, I'm at — '

A hand tore the telephone from her grasp; she saw the flash of a knife in the light, and the wire dangled free from the wall!

'I'll kill you for that,' cried the Hooded Terror, and caught her in his arms . . . but Christine never heard him, as she had fainted!

16

Two Shots

For a second Dick stood by the telephone motionless, his heart beating thunderously, while Cowles and Morrison stared at him, their faces white and drawn. He felt a sudden sensation of sickness. It had been Christine's voice, and as long as he lived he would never forget the terror-laden appeal of it.

Inspector Cowles was the first to break the tense silence. 'There's not a moment to lose,' he snapped. 'We must find out the origin of that call.'

Dick made an effort to control his emotions and pulled the telephone towards him, moving the hook up and down impatiently.

'Hello,' he called. 'Hello . . . Confound it, have they all gone to sleep at the Exchange? . . . Hello! Put me on to inquiries at once. Scotland Yard speaking. It's very urgent.'

He looked at Cowles while he waited for a reply, and his face was haggard and strained. 'I doubt if we can find her in time,' he groaned huskily. 'He must have surprised her in the act of phoning, and the swine cut the wire. What's happening now, God only knows!'

He addressed himself again to the telephone. 'Hello! Hello! . . . Why in heaven's name can't they hurry up?' His hand holding the receiver shook in spite of his efforts to control himself.

'There's no sense in getting in a panic, old man,' said Cowles. 'Oh, I know how you feel about it,' he added as Dick uttered an impatient exclamation. 'I'm feeling pretty rotten myself. But you've got to drum it into your head that the girl's all right. If you allow yourself to think any other way, you'll be incapable of anything.' He himself was feeling the strain, and found it almost insupportable.

'It's terrible — terrible,' said Morrison. 'To think of Christine in the clutches of that brute . . . ' He sunk his head in his hands and groaned.

Cowles glared at him. 'For heaven's

sake, don't let your nerve go, Morrison,' he rapped sharply. 'Pull yourself together, man. We're none of us going to do any good by imagining horrors. The only thing that is going to save the girl is action and clear-headedness.' He sounded callous, but he was right and they knew it.

'Is that enquiries?' cried Dick at last. 'Yes . . . A call was put through to me here a few minutes ago. I want to know where it originated . . . To Dick Trent, yes, at Scotland Yard . . . Hurry as quick as you can — it's urgent!'

There was another wait, and Dick sat motionless, staring at the desk in front of him with eyes that saw nothing but the picture of a fair-haired, laughing girl in a dress of black charmeuse.

Morrison had risen from his chair and was pacing monotonously to and fro. Cowles remained outwardly calm, but inwardly he was seething with excitement and anger against the man who had been responsible for the abduction of the girl.

None of them spoke. Each was too occupied with his own gloomy thoughts.

After what seemed like centuries, but

was in reality only a few minutes, Dick got a reply from enquiries in answer to his questions. 'Yes,' he cried into the mouthpiece while his hand sought for and found a pencil. 'One-Tree Farm, Meopham in Kent.' He jotted down the answer on a pad at his elbow. 'What is the subscriber's name? Ellistone . . . Thank you.'

He hung up the receiver and sprang to his feet, pressing the bell on his desk as he did so. 'Come along,' he said tersely, and Cowles was surprised at the sudden steadiness of his voice. 'Christine's at a place called One-Tree Farm in Meopham.'

A sergeant entered in answer to Dick's summons. 'I want the fastest car you can get hold of,' rapped Dick quickly, turning to the man, 'and the shortest route to Meopham. And I want it in three minutes.'

The sergeant nodded stolidly, saluted and hurried away to execute the order. Dick opened a drawer in his desk and took out two ugly-looking automatics, and examined the magazines.

'Who's Ellistone?' asked Cowles.

'I know who Ellistone is,' answered Dick. 'There's a big surprise coming to you — if we're not too late. Are you armed?' Cowles shook his head. 'Well, take one of these.' Dick handed him a pistol. 'You'll need it. I know you're armed, Morrison,' he added.

'I haven't been without a pistol in my pocket for the last five years,' said Morrison grimly. 'I carry two, and when I meet Hammer Stevens two aren't going to be enough!'

'Come on, then,' said Dick, and he took a leather driving coat from a cupboard.

They followed him down the stairs and into the street. It was less than three minutes since Dick had issued his order, but the car was ready. It was a big high-powered Daimler, and was capable of a speed of over eighty miles an hour. Cowles eyed it approvingly as Dick took his place at the wheel. The sergeant had carried out his instructions to the letter, and to the wheel was fixed a map with the route marked in red ink. Cowles got in beside Dick, and

Morrison climbed into the back.

Dick turned to the sergeant as the car began to move forward. 'Put a call through and clear the roads for me,' he shouted. 'I don't want to be held up while I waste time explaining, and I'm going to break all the speed limits that were ever made today.'

The next moment they had started their journey with a fervent prayer that they would not arrive too late.

Through London Dick had to keep the speed of the great car down, but once past the outskirts he pressed his foot down hard upon the accelerator and kept it there. So smoothly did the car travel that Morrison could scarcely believe that it was travelling at nearly seventy miles an hour, until leaning forward in his seat he saw the steadily moving finger of the speed indicator.

The whine of the wind rose to a shrill hum as it tore past their ears, and the rain stung their faces like the lashes of a thousand tiny nails. Once, rounding a corner, the car skidded on the wet surface of the road, but Dick skilfully saved it from disaster and they rushed on.

For miles the countryside flashed by as one continuous green blur, changing its hue for a moment as the car roared through small towns and villages.

The road they were travelling remained practically empty, but as they neared Chislehurst a huge lorry suddenly emerged from a side lane, and for a second Cowles felt his heart leap into his throat. It appeared that nothing could save them from crashing into it. But Dick never hesitated. In a flash he realized the danger, and the impossibility of pulling up in time at the speed they were going. With an iron nerve he sent the Daimler forward, all out!

A twist of the wheel at the right moment, and the car shot between the lumbering lorry and the side bank of the road, with hardly an inch to spare on either side. But that inch was as good as a mile, and the disaster was averted.

St. Mary Cray and Swanley were passed and left behind, and they were nearing Farningham, when suddenly there was a loud report and a tyre burst!

The car swerved and nearly ran off the side of the road, but Dick pulled frantically at the wheel and got her nose straight again, continuing on a flat tyre. He brought the speed down appreciably, and he grew hot and cold as the mileage dropped, but there was no time to waste changing the wheel.

To the rhythmic sound of the engine hammered the thought in his mind, would he be in time? Would he be in time? Over and over again . . .

The mad race was nearing its end when they passed Fawkham and tore on toward Meopham. The burst tyre caused the car to rock and sway. Cowles and Morrison had to grip the sides of the seats to keep themselves from being jerked out. At Meopham Station Dick brought the car to a halt and, leaning out, called to a bucolic-looking youth who was lounging outside: 'Which is the way to One-Tree Farm?'

The youth stared at him with bulging eyes, and scratched his head.

'Come on, quickly,' cried Dick impatiently.

But the boy was not to be hurried. Slowly and laboriously he directed them, and Dick had wasted five precious minutes before he gained the information he required and sent the car tearing off again.

The route lead them up a narrow road overhung with trees which was evidently little used, for the car bumped and swayed over the road surface. The boy had told them to take the first turning on the left, and Dick nearly missed it, so nearly hidden was the lane by the overgrown hedge.

This road was worse than the other, but presently as he rounded a bend, Dick gave vent to a little cry of triumph. Close to a broken fence stood a large black limousine! Cowles and Morrison saw it at the same instant. With the front lamps of the Daimler almost touching the back of the other car, Dick brought it to a stop and sprang from his seat. As he did so, he uttered a cry of astonishment.

In front of the limousine was a third car — a little open sports two-seater. He raced up to it. On the wet driving seat lay a woman's glove! Dick picked it up and looked at Cowles in wonder. 'He's got a woman with him!' he exclaimed. 'Who the deuce can she be, and why didn't she travel in the other car?'

'Perhaps the glove belongs to Miss Baker,' suggested Cowles.

Dick held it for a second to his nostrils and shook his head. 'She doesn't use this kind of perfume,' he said.

'Why waste time?' interposed Morrison. 'Let's find the house; it must be close here.' He opened a gate in the fence. 'This is the way the boy said — across this footpath to that clump of trees.' He set off at a run along the muddy track, followed by Dick and Inspector Cowles. From behind the trees ahead there suddenly appeared a thick column of black smoke. Dick pointed to it as he raced along.

'It looks as if the place is on fire!' he panted.

Halfway across the field they stopped dead and looked at each other, and Dick's heart almost ceased to beat. From somewhere in front came the sound of two shots, distinct and clear, fired in rapid succession, and followed by a woman's scream!

17

The Revelation

Christine must have remained unconscious for a considerable time, but all the while she had a peculiar sensation of being dimly aware of what was happening. It was as though her subconscious mind remained active after her conscious mind had deserted her. As in a dream, she felt herself lifted up and carried. Then she was laid on something soft and yielding. Presently she felt some sort of cold liquid trickling down her face. Then everything went black again. She seemed to be falling from a great height — down — down — down. She put up her hands to save herself, and recovered her senses.

She found that she was lying on the sofa in the sitting room, and the masked man was bathing her head with water. As she opened her eyes he stooped and held a glass to her lips. 'Drink this!' he ordered.

The ice-cold water almost completely restored her, and she struggled to a sitting position.

'I made up my mind to kill you,' said the Hooded Terror, 'when I discovered that you were trying to betray me. But I have changed my plans. I want you; you are necessary to me. I couldn't do without you now. But by your act you have endangered my safety, and we must leave here at once. It will not be long before Trent discovers that the phone call came from here and sets out in search of you.' He must have seen the hope that suddenly lit up her eyes, for he continued, 'But he will not find you. We shall have gone before he can possibly get here. I would sooner kill you, and myself too, than hand you over to any other man. You understand? I would sooner see you dead! That is an alternative for you to remember.'

'There are worse things than death,' she replied steadily, although her whole being was suffused with fear.

He looked at her in silence; then, turning, he crossed to the sideboard. He unlocked a drawer and presently came back to her side, carrying a black leather case. 'I hoped that this would not be necessary,' he remarked as he opened it and removed the shining instrument it contained.

At the sight of the hypodermic syringe, Christine shrank back. 'What — what are you going to do?' she asked faintly.

'I am merely taking a precaution to ensure that there will be no more telephone incidents,' he answered, calmly removing the cork from a small phial containing a colourless liquid.

A wild spasm of terror shot through her heart as she realized his intention. 'Not that, not that,' she begged. 'Anything but that!'

He paused, and his eyes through the slits in the cowl regarded her steadily. 'Will you swear, then,' he said, 'that you will make no attempt to escape?'

'Yes, yes,' she cried eagerly, watching the horrible instrument in his hand. 'I promise you.'

He paused for a moment in thought. 'I'll trust you,' he said at last. 'I'm probably a fool, but I'll trust you. But if you try to betray me again, you will not live to witness the success of your plans.' He broke off sharply. 'What was that?'

She had heard nothing. He stood, his head bent forward, listening tensely. 'I thought I heard someone moving about outside the window,' he said. 'Wait here.'

He hurried from the room, and she noticed that he did not trouble to lock the door. He had accepted her promise without question. What had he heard that had startled him? She listened. Presently she heard him moving about among the bushes that grew close up to the front of the cottage.

Would Dick arrive before the Hooded Terror had taken her away? If once they left the cottage, the likelihood of her ever being traced was remote. Her only hope was to delay the departure as long as possible. Curiously, she never thought of breaking her promise. Although she hated the masked man with a loathing beyond description — seeing in him the ugly reality — and her soul shrank in horror from the prospect he had opened up to her, yet she had given her word, and she meant to stick to it.

His real alternative to marriage she knew and understood only too well. His plan was to degrade her so that she would never be able to hold up her head or meet Dick's tender eyes. So that she would in desperation agree to anything to save her name from disgrace. She made up her mind that sooner than that, she would die by her own hand.

She heard him returning. 'It was nothing,' he said as he entered. 'It must have been my imagination. It's time we were going. We've wasted too long already.' He laid his hand on her shoulder, and his touch sent a shudder of dread through her. He must have noticed it, but he made no comment, and handed to her the hat and coat which he had removed when she fainted.

Christine was thinking quickly. In some way or other she must gain time — time to give Dick a chance of reaching her. 'Can I wash?' she asked calmly.

He hesitated for a moment, and then nodded. 'You will have to hurry,' he said, and led the way along the passage to the kitchen. He found a towel and handed it to her. 'You will find water and soap in there.' He pointed to a small scullery that opened out of the kitchen. A bucket of crystal-clear well water stood on a table, and she bathed her face and hands and felt refreshed. The masked man stood watching her impatiently.

'Where are we going?' she asked as she finished her hurried toilet.

'I'm afraid I can't tell you that,' he replied. 'You will have to possess your soul in patience, and wait.' There was a glitter in his eyes that frightened her.

What was his plan now? she wondered. What fresh scheme had he evolved?

It was the brain behind that horrible mask that terrified her. That cool, calculating brain that had planned her abduction so neatly and with such minute care, and had for so long baffled all the officials at Scotland Yard.

'I cannot wait any longer,' he said. 'I am running a great risk now. We must go.'

He took her arm and pushed her along the passage. At the front door he paused. 'I have one more thing to do here,' he said, and picked up a square tin from the floor. He disappeared for a second into the sitting room, and she smelled the strong fumes of petrol as they wafted down the passage. She heard a sudden roar and he reappeared, shutting the sitting room door quickly behind him.

'Fire destroys all traces,' he remarked as he hurriedly unbarred the front door, and she understood!

It was broad daylight outside, and he hurried her down the little path to the gate by which she had entered.

She was racking her brains desperately to think of some plan to delay their departure, but she could think of nothing. Her heart sank in despair. As they rounded the bushes and came in sight of the gate, she looked back. Already the cottage was in flames, and as a dense column of smoke was ascending to the sky, it seemed as if all her hopes were going with it.

'In a short while, Christine,' said the

Hooded Terror, 'you will know me for who I am, for I cannot travel in daylight with this thing upon my head.'

He had dropped his unnatural, high-pitched, squeaky voice, and spoke for the first time in his natural tones. Christine felt her heart give a leap, for she recognized the voice!

'My heavens, is it you?' she cried, recoiling from him.

He raised his hands and tore the cowl from his head. 'Yes, it's I!' he cried, and caught the shrinking girl in his arms. 'We are standing on the threshold of a new life, Christine, and — '

'You are standing on the threshold of death!' cried a voice. 'Let go that girl, Stevens, and take what's coming to you!'

Christine felt the arms about her slacken and, twisting herself free, turned to face the direction from which the voice had come. Then she gave a cry of astonishment. A woman stood by a clump of bushes. Her untidy hair hung in draggled wisps over her forehead, and her clothes were soaked and mud-spattered. In her hand she held an ugly automatic pistol, which she pointed steadily at the Hooded Terror.

'Keep back!' he screamed, a note of fear in his voice.

'You know what I've come for,' cried Lydia, with a look in her eyes that froze Christine's blood. 'You murderer! You killed Harry. Killed him because he knew you for who you were. He was in the next cell to you at Dartmoor.'

'Keep back!' he cried again, and his hand moved so quickly that the girl could not follow it. 'Take that!' he cried.

Two shots rang out almost together, and Christine screamed.

The Hooded Terror staggered and fell, tried to struggle to his feet, and then with a little choking sob pitched forward on his face, his arms outstretched, his clawing hands digging into the soft gravel.

Lydia threw away her pistol and put her arm round the frightened girl. 'You're all right now,' she said soothingly, and at the words Christine's strained nerves gave way and she sobbed on the other woman's shoulder.

It was thus that Dick found them as he

came tearing up the path a moment later, followed by Cowles and Morrison. 'What's happened?' he cried, an agony of apprehension in his voice. Then, as his eyes took in the scene, he understood.

At the sound of his voice Christine raised her head with a glad cry, and the next instant she was in his arms.

'You can take me, Trent,' said Lydia defiantly. 'I shot him.'

'Who is it?' asked Dick in a low voice.

'The Hooded Terror,' answered Lydia. 'His real name was Henry Stevens.'

Cowles pursed his lips thoughtfully, and his eyes rested on the still figure on the ground.

'Is he quite dead?' asked Jack Morrison.

The inspector knelt down by the side of the body and turned it over, and as he did so he gave a great cry of astonishment. The dead face, staring with sightless eyes at the sky, was the face of James Lathbury!

18

Morrison's Story

The sitting room at Christine Baker's flat presented a cosy appearance. The remains of a substantial meal that had been sent in from a neighboring restaurant still occupied the table, and around the fire were gathered the little group of people who had just partaken of it. They consisted of Richard Trent, Detective Cowles, Christine Baker and Last Minute Morrison.

'Now,' said Dick, looking across at Morrison, who was sprawling in an easy chair, the picture of lazy contentment, 'I think it is up to you to do a little explaining. There are several blanks that I would like you to fill in.'

Morrison raised his eyes and winked deliberately at Christine, who was seated on the tiny sofa by Dick's side. 'You see,' he murmured with a smile, 'the police cannot get on for long without the press. Even a high official of Scotland Yard has in the end to turn to a humble reporter for information.' He settled himself more comfortably in his chair. 'Well, here goes,' he said resignedly, and began his story.

'My real name is John Arkwright, and I might as well state here and now that I am, by all moral standards, a criminal, although I have not been guilty of any criminal act for considerably over fifteen years. Gordon Arkwright was my brother, and my elder by nearly eight years. Both our parents died when we were little more than children, and we were left without money to fend for ourselves. There is no occasion for me to go into details of our early life; it has no connection with that which I am about to tell you. It is sufficient if I say that at the age when most boys are thinking about games and schooling, we were devising ways and means of putting food into our hungry stomachs.

'Gradually we became drawn into a set that, to say the least, was not good for our youthful morals; and by the time I had reached the early twenties we were out for anything that was likely to put money into our pockets, irrespective of right or wrong.'

He paused for a moment and stared thoughtfully at the fire, as if seeking inspiration from its cheerful flames. 'Don't think,' he continued presently, 'that I am offering this as an excuse for my misdeeds. Nothing is further from my mind. I am merely stating plain facts, and it is absolutely necessary that you should know them in order to understand what happened afterward.

'As soon as I became old enough to think, I began to get fed up with the kind of life I was leading, and I decided to cut it all out and go abroad. After some difficulty I managed to get a job with a fur-trading company and went to Canada. The work was hard, and the hours long, but I thoroughly enjoyed it, and the only regret I had was at having to leave my brother, Gordon. Between us two there was a bond of affection stronger, I think, than is usually found among brothers, particularly on my side, and I put this down to the fact that Gordon, being the elder, had practically brought me up. I know that I absolutely worshipped him, and in my eyes he was little less than a tin god.

'I had been nearly a year in Canada when the firm for which I was working suddenly went bankrupt, and I found myself out of a job. I didn't mind so much at first, for I had managed to save a little money; but as the weeks went by and my savings gradually diminished and I was still out of work, I began to realize that things were getting serious. I was sitting in my room one night, trying to make up my mind what was the best thing to do, when the post brought me a letter from Gordon. He wrote saying that he had struck a wonderfully paying game, and that with my assistance we could both make more than a comfortable income. In a nutshell, it amounted to this: Gordon had become a receiver of stolen goods — a fence, I believe is the correct term; and his idea was to pass the stuff he had got into his possession on to me in Canada so that it could be disposed of more easily, and without any risk of it being traced.

'To cut a long story short, I agreed to the proposition, and for years we carried on the business, my bank balance steadily increasing as time went by. There was little risk attached, for Gordon specialized in stolen bank notes, the numbers of which were known. He would send them to me; I would pass them and return other notes in their place; and after deducting a third of their original value, the balance was handed by Gordon to the person who originally stole them. His method of getting them out to me was to conceal them inside the covers of new novels, and not once during the entire period of our operations were they ever discovered. The whole of the notes stolen by Hammer Stevens from the Trans-Atlantic Bank I received in this way and passed successfully, but in the meantime Stevens was arrested and sentenced before his share of the money could be handed over to him.

'Shortly after that Gordon married. I never saw his wife, of course, but from the photograph he sent me at the time I imagine she must have been a very lovely girl.' His eyes dwelt for a moment on Christine. She was leaning slightly forward, gazing steadily at him, listening eagerly to every word that dropped from his lips.

'Gordon never told his wife how he made his money,' continued Morrison, 'and his greatest anxiety was that she should find out. A year passed, and then came the tragedy that soured his life and made him an old man before his time. His wife died in giving birth to a child — a girl. Gordon never recovered from the shock, and almost immediately afterward, he gave up his house in London and moved to a dilapidated old farm on the borders of Dartmoor, from which on a clear day he said it was possible to see the convict prison at Princetown.

'About this time, Scotland Yard, who had been greatly concerned for some time as to how the notes stolen in big robberies had been successfully negotiated, became suspicious of Gordon. I don't know what turned their attention to him, for we had taken every precaution to guard against discovery, but they set detectives on to watch him. Gordon became aware of this, and fearing that he might be in danger of arrest at any moment, he wrote to me asking if I would take charge of his little girl, who was then about eight months old. I readily agreed, and he arranged for little Christine to be sent out to me in Canada in charge of a nurse. It was Gordon's express wish that she should not be known by her real name of Arkwright, so that, should he be arrested and convicted, no stigma could ever be attached to the child. So she was sent in the name of Christine Baker.'

'Why is it you've never told me this before?' asked Christine, her voice trembling slightly.

'Because,' answered Morrison gently, 'it was unnecessary. It would not have made you any happier to have known, and it might have caused you a lot of needless pain and worry.

'Three years passed,' he went on, 'and during that time Gordon lived in almost hourly fear of discovery. Although as it turned out his fears were groundless, for the police were unable to unearth a scrap of evidence sufficient to warrant his arrest. The money I had made during my association with Gordon I had invested carefully, and I was fairly well off; so, being anxious to see my brother again, I decided one day to return to England. There was no further need for me to remain in Canada, since Gordon, directly he found that he was suspected, had dropped all his dealings. I wrote to him, telling him of my intention, and saying that I had reserved my passage and was sailing on the next boat which left in three days' time, and bringing Christine, who was then nearly six years old, with me. I arrived in London two days after the escape of Hammer Stevens from Prince-town Prison, and learned from the papers of his supposed murder at the hands of Gordon.

'From the first I never believed that Gordon was guilty. Knowing him as well as I did, I knew that he was absolutely incapable of committing such a crime, particularly in the brutal way the papers stated. But if he had not killed Stevens, who had? Also, why had Gordon disappeared? It suddenly occurred to me how easy the whole thing would be to explain if the positions were reversed and it had been Gordon who had been killed, not Hammer Stevens.

'I determined to put my theory — and the more I thought of it, the more I became convinced it was the true one — to the test. Assuming the guise of a freelance reporter, which enabled me to conduct my enquiries without arousing attention, I set out to make my investigations. It is unnecessary for me to go into details concerning all my inquiries. The greatest stumbling block in the way of my theory was that the body had already been identified as that of Stevens. I managed, however, to obtain permission to view the body; and immediately, in spite of the fact that the face had been mutilated beyond recognition, I knew instinctively that it was Gordon.'

'But,' interposed Cowles, 'it was identified by the governor of the prison himself.'

Morrison shook his head. 'It was not,' he said. 'The real governor was ill at the time, and it was his deputy who identified the body — a man who, I discovered, had only seen Stevens once or twice in his life.'

'Why didn't you inform the police of your suspicions?' asked Dick.

'I think the reason is fairly obvious,' answered Morrison. 'It would have led to a lot of enquiries, and I had no desire for the police to investigate my private affairs too closely. If they had discovered that Gordon had a brother, and that brother had just arrived from Canada, they could easily have put two and two together and discovered the means by which the notes had been passed — and that would have meant my arrest for receiving stolen property.'

'I see,' said Dick, nodding.

'To return to my story,' Morrison continued, 'I knew now that my brother had been murdered by Hammer Stevens, and a cold rage against this man took possession of me. I determined to devote the rest of my life, if necessary, to finding him and exacting vengeance.

'I managed after a good deal of trouble to trace him as far as Truro, and in the room which he had occupied I found a clue which eventually put me on his track. It was a very slight one, and merely consisted of a scrap of paper which had been scribbled all over with tiny circles in pencil. The landlord told me that the man had had a habit of scribbling like this on any old paper that happened to be handy when he was thinking. From Truro I succeeded in tracing him to London, and here I lost him altogether. Somehow or other he must have discovered who it was that was on his track, for on two occasions attempts were made on my life.

'Nearly fourteen years passed, and during that time I never once gave up my search for Hammer Stevens. The guise I had adopted in the first place, that of a reporter, gave me an idea. I decided to adopt the profession, for it seemed to me that it was one in which I stood the best chance of finding the man I was after. So I obtained a job on the *Monitor*, changing my name to that of Jack

Morrison, and, as you know, I gradually worked my way up until I was in the position I now hold.

'Christine, in the meanwhile, had been sent to school, retaining the name I had given her of Baker, and entirely ignorant of her parentage. I merely told her in answer to her questions that they had died when she was a baby — which, of course, was true.

'Then came the first outrage perpetrated by the Hooded Terror: the robbery of the Western and Union Bank and the murder of the night watchman. I was given the job of writing it up for the *Monitor*, and I went to interview the manager, James Lathbury. While I was talking to him I noticed with a shock that throughout our conversation he was drawing innumerable little penciled circles on the blotting pad in front of him! At first I thought it merely a coincidence; it seemed impossible that a man in Lathbury's position could be the man I was in search of. But it was worthwhile following up, and I decided in the future to keep Lathbury under observation.

'Christine had left college for some time, and at my interview with Lathbury I had learnt that he was in search of a secretary. Through the influence of a man I knew in the banking world, I managed to get Christine the situation. I never imagined for one moment that she would be in any danger, and as Lathbury's private secretary, she would be in the position to let me know many particulars concerning his private affairs. Of course, she had no idea of my real objective, for I had informed her that I was merely investigating the finances of the Western and Union Bank on behalf of the *Monitor*. This was quite plausible, because as you remember, just before Lathbury took control the bank was in a very parlous state.

'I watched and waited; and gradually, partly from the information given me by Christine and partly from my own discoveries, I became convinced that James Lathbury and Hammer Stevens were one and the same person. It was quite a plausible theory. I had read up all records of Hammer Stevens's life, and I knew that he had made a specialty of banks and had the whole business at his fingertips.

'I had installed Christine in a flat with strict instructions that she was not to divulge our relationship, giving as my reason that the *Monitor* did not wish anyone to know that I was making investigations concerning the stability of the Western and Union Bank, and that, if the fact became known that she was my niece, and acting as Lathbury's secretary, it might give rise to suspicion.

'In order to study Lathbury at close quarters I opened an account at the bank, and after a little while had elapsed I had a third interview with him, making the excuse that I wished to arrange an overdraft. Although I was by now fairly certain in my own mind that I had found Hammer Stevens at last, I could obtain no definite proof to bear out my suspicions. I approached the editor of the *Monitor*, and so that I could devote the whole of my time to obtaining the proofs I needed, asked his permission to undertake the job of discovering the identity of the Hooded Terror. He readily granted my request. Almost immediately afterward came the murder of Blackie Phrynne. I made enquiries and discovered that Lathbury had been absent from his house at the exact time that Phrynne was killed at the door of Dick's flat.'

'Why didn't you take us into your confidence?' asked Dick.

'I had nothing to go on,' replied Morrison. 'Only a vague suspicion. I had told you then who I believed the Hooded Terror was, you'd only have laughed at me.

'It was a clever move on Lathbury's part to make his first big operation the robbery of his own bank, for it put him absolutely beyond suspicion. After thinking the matter over carefully, I came to the conclusion that the only possible way of bringing his guilt home to him was to obtain some documentary evidence that he was the Hooded Terror. The cards bearing the stamped impression of the black cowled head — which were characteristic of all Hooded Terror crimes — must be kept somewhere, and I concluded that the most likely place would, in all probability, be the safe at his private residence. That was when I determined, on a bold stroke, nothing less than to break into Lathbury's house and search for them.

'I approached Christine and arranged for her to meet me there in the garden at the back of the house, and told her that in order to conclude my inquiries for the *Monitor* it was necessary that I should resort to means that were not strictly legal. My idea was that she would be able to keep watch outside and warn me should anything occur that was likely to lead to my discovery. She got there before her time and, while waiting for me to arrive, was dismayed to see a strange man climb the low wall into the garden. She became frightened and ran away. I had been delayed, owing to having to finish a special article for the *Monitor* which they were waiting for to go to press, and when I arrived at Lathbury's house it was to discover to my surprise all the lights on. I went round to the back and, seeing no signs of Christine, I concluded that she had given up waiting for me, had been scared by the sight of the lighted house, and gone home. Nobody was more astonished than I when I learned of the robbery.'

'Of course,' said Dick, 'Wallace broke in with the same object as you. He was searching for proof to confirm his suspicions, and according to his wife's story, he apparently found it. He must have seen Lathbury in London, recognized him as the Hammer Stevens who had occupied the next cell to him at Dartmoor, discovered who he was, and saw in his discovery a chance of easy money — as he thought, poor devil — by blackmailing Lathbury.'

Morrison agreed. 'Of course, at the time I had no knowledge of this,' he continued. 'My plan having failed, I decided that the only thing I could do was to keep close watch on Lathbury's movements. This I did, and, as you already know, on the night when Christine was abducted I had followed him as far as her flat. If he hadn't discovered me and attacked me with a life preserver, I should have been able to prevent him carrying out his damnable plan. Christine had told me that Lathbury had proposed to her, and I instantly advised her to give in her notice at the bank; but I never had any idea that she was in any danger, or that he would go to the lengths he did.

'I think that's about all,' he concluded. 'Everything else you know.'

There was a thoughtful silence, which was broken at length by Cowles. 'Of course, Lathbury left the card on his own desk in order to turn suspicion away from himself,' he remarked. 'But what about the envelope containing the list of securities? Did Wallace take that?'

'He didn't,' answered Morrison, 'for the simple reason that it was never at Lathbury's house to take. Directly you mentioned the matter to me, I asked Christine, and she told me that he had never taken it home at all.'

'Then, why,' said Dick, 'did he say it had been stolen?'

'I think,' replied Morrison, 'that he was beginning to get a trifle suspicious of me. I don't think he ever connected me with

Gordon's brother, but I think he was afraid that I was getting to know too much, and by saying that the envelope containing a list of my securities had been the only thing stolen, he would subtly throw suspicion on me.'

'By Jove! He succeeded for a time,' said Cowles, laughing. 'For at one time I was almost convinced that you were the Hooded Terror.'

'There's just one thing you don't know,' said Morrison. 'I was present at a meeting between the Hooded Terror and his gang, hidden unknown to them, when he finally broke up the organization. I can give you a list of most of the members — not that it matters very much, for they'll be practically helpless without the leading brain behind them; but some of the names will surprise you.'

Christine, who had been staring, silent and motionless, into the fire, turned to Dick. 'What is going to happen to that poor woman?' she enquired softly. 'You're surely not going to arrest her for what she did?'

'I don't think so,' replied Dick. 'I owe

her far too much. Her shooting of Stevens can be recorded as self-defense — he shot at her but missed. She's going abroad to try and forget everything and start afresh.'

'I hope she succeeds,' said Cowles. 'There's a lot of good in Lydia, if she'd only let it come out.'

'And what about me?' said Morrison, turning to Dick with a twinkle in his eye. 'I suppose you know that, having convicted myself with my own lips, you're at perfect liberty to arrest me.'

'I don't think it will be necessary,' replied Dick. 'And besides, I should hate to have a convict for a relation. It would look so bad at the Yard!' And he turned to Christine with a smile.

We do hope that you have enjoyed reading this large print book.

Did you know that all of our titles are available for purchase?

We publish a wide range of high quality large print books including:
Romances, Mysteries, Classics
General Fiction
Non Fiction and Westerns

Special interest titles available in large print are:
The Little Oxford Dictionary
Music Book, Song Book
Hymn Book, Service Book

Also available from us courtesy of Oxford University Press:
Young Readers' Dictionary
(large print edition)
Young Readers' Thesaurus
(large print edition)

For further information or a free brochure, please contact us at:
Ulverscroft Large Print Books Ltd.,
The Green, Bradgate Road, Anstey,
Leicester, LE7 7FU, England.
Tel: (00 44) **0116 236 4325**
Fax: (00 44) **0116 234 0205**

Other titles in the
Linford Mystery Library:

THE CLASSIC CAR KILLER

Richard A. Lupoff

The members of the New California Smart Set love to dress in the fashions of the 1920s and dance to the music of that bygone era. They even bring out a magnificent vintage limousine for display at their annual gala — which is promptly stolen. Insurance investigator Hobart Lindsey is called upon to unravel an intricate puzzle that soon leads to brutal murder and an attempt on his own life. Aided by his streetwise police officer girlfriend Marvia Plum, the unlikely partners are off on another hazardous adventure!

GRAVE WATERS

Ana R. Morlan and Mary W. Burgess

Two cunning, cold-blooded killers board the cruise ship *Nerissa* disguised as an elderly couple, with a deadly armoury at their disposal courtesy of the Russian Mafia. Meanwhile, members of a mysterious cult called the Foundation have infiltrated the passenger list, with their own sinister agenda to take over the ship. When they strike, they disrupt the on-board wedding ceremony of police officer David Spaulding. Can the ship's captain, aided by David and his new friend, author and anthropologist Richard Black Wolf, regain control of the *Nerissa* before it's too late?

THE OTHER MRS. WATSON

Michael Mallory

Who was the elusive second wife of John Watson, trusted friend and chronicler of the great Sherlock Holmes? The secret is now revealed in *The Other Mrs. Watson*, eight stories featuring Amelia Watson, devoted and opinionated wife of the good doctor, and intrepid (if a bit reluctant) amateur sleuth. Jack the Ripper is back, and up to his old tricks . . . Ghosts and demons materialise to trouble the living . . . An old acquaintance of Holmes's reappears, with cut-throats on her tail . . . And murder seems to lurk around every corner!

MISSION: THIRD FORCE

Michael Kurland

In the late 1960s, the Cold War threatens the survival of mankind. To help keep the uneasy peace, a new group of mercenaries is born: known as Weapons Analysis and Research, Incorporated. Whilst WAR, Inc. does not supply fighting troops, it provides training, equipment, systems, advice and technical expertise ... Now former major Peter Carthage leads his men into the hostile jungles of Bonterre to prevent the overthrow of its government by guerrillas — and the mysterious Third Force known only as 'X' ...